Praise for *The Last Summer*

*I instantly felt a connection to Charley as the heroine, rooting for her through the days of summer, as she struggled with both the internal and external changes faced by a teenage girl. **The Last Summer** is, without question, a novel I would recommend for my classroom library and one that would capture the attention of junior high students, both boys and girls alike. Jacky's talent for writing surpasses the ordinary to the extraordinary.*

—KATHLEEN FALK, JD 8th Grade Teacher, St. Mary School

'Professor Jacky' takes us on a wonderful field trip into a past that is rich with historical significance. We discover through the lives of these eloquently drawn characters a time in which friendship was a treasured find and love still held the magic of innocence. And in many ways, this story gives voice to a new generation whose values signal a rebirth of such a time.

-DR. ROBERT MCTYRE. SR.

Jacquelyn Eubanks has an exceptional first book – plotting, development of characters and creating her little Georgia town marks this author for future greatness.

-ROBERT PENDERGAST
Lima, Fort Wayne, Chicago Newsman

Eubanks is a writer far beyond her years with the ability to capture the reader's attention and interest from the get-go. The maturity in her written word and story-telling ability is apparent throughout. 'The Last Summer' is a page-turner that is sure to resonate with young adults and mature audiences alike. Set in a small town in the mid-1950s, 'The Last Summer' is an adventurous tale that explores the peculiarities of childhood including friendship, family, personal beliefs and young love. The relatable characters, dynamic relationships and touching storyline yield an impressive glimpse into the inner workings of a young girl finding her footing as she faces a move from the place she has come to call home.

-ALISON CAVATORE

CEO & Founder of Global Living Magazine

To Katie

THE *Last* Summer

Jacquelyn Eubanks

By Jacquelyn Eubanks

VG Publishing. Chesterfield, Michigan

ISBN: 0978590031
ISBN-13: 9780978590031
Library of Congress Catalog Number: 2011938046

CONTENTS

June 1948

The Beginning of the Beginning

Our Oldsmobile pulled up in front of a small two-story house on the left side of the road. My father tentatively backed into the driveway as I fidgeted in the backseat, bouncing around, trying to get a good view of my new home. The house looked quiet and lonely. I was not as excited to move in as I had been five minutes ago.

Father shut off the engine and got out of the car. He opened my mother's door to let her out, giving me the feeling that it was high time I got out, too. I'd sat far too long in that car, and all I wanted was to take advantage of my new house's indoor plumbing.

Flash forward a few minutes, I'd exited the bathroom and was sent to help move boxes up to my bedroom. After only a couple moments, however, I had proven myself "too much of an obstacle" and was forced to sit on the porch, doing nothing.

Out of nowhere a boy about my age appeared in the front yard of the house directly across the street from me. Gosh, he sure was cute! The cutest boy I'd ever seen, in fact.

I jumped up and rushed over to him. He looked at me curiously. I just smiled.

"Hi!" I said. "My name's Charley."

"No it ain't. Charlie's a boy's name," he responded.

"Nuh-*uh*. Charley is short for my real name, Charlotte. Only special people get to call me Charley. Like my Grandpa." In my mind I added, "*and you can too.*"

"Well, I'm Frankie. I just turned eight on May 16th. How old are you?"

"I'll be eight on July 29th." I notice he's wearing a baseball mitt.

"Hey! Look! We *both* like baseball!" I grin, pointing to the New York Yankees baseball cap on my head.

"I don't like baseball," he frowns. My heart sinks with disappointment. "I LOVE it!" he exclaims. I instantly cheer up.

"Well? What are we waiting for? Let's go play!" I shout excitedly.

"Okay. We can play in my backyard. You can borrow my mitt for now." He hands me his mitt as I follow him into his backyard. He picks an old mitt and baseball off the ground and we start playing catch. This kid is amazing! Every throw and catch he makes is perfect.

"You're too good to be a girl. You play like all of my friends," he says nicely. "You should meet them. I'm sure they'd like having you play baseball games with us all summer."

"Oh, thanks! Me and Grandpa used to practice a lot, until we moved away from New York."

"New York?! That's where the Yankees play!"

"I know! They're my favorite team!"

"No way! Mine too!" We play in happy silence for a long while.

Suddenly I hear an unfamiliar girl voice calling my name.

"Charlotte! Charlotte! Charlotte! Where are you?! *Charlotte*!" A pretty blonde girl who looks about the same age as me runs through the open backyard gate. Fear and worry's crawling all over her face like spiders on a web. She stops short and looks quickly from me to Frankie and back again. Then she screams in outrage.

CHAPTER 1

The First Day of Summer

Summer 1955

"This is going to be the best summer ever. I can tell," I state matter-of-factly to my two best friends. The three of us are hiking up a green, grassy hill, trying to make our way over it to the other side.

"And *how*, exactly, do you know that?" Arthur asks, raising one eyebrow, forever being the analytical one of the group.

"I don't *know* it. I just...*feel* it," I explain, pulling off my trademark New York Yankees baseball cap to wipe the sweat off my brow with my forearm.

"Kinda like how you *feel* the need to shove me in the arm whenever I tease you?" Frankie comments sarcastically, so I playfully elbow him in the side.

The sky is a deep and rich blue, spotted by only a few small white clouds in the distance. There's a refreshing breeze to keep the mid-morning cool, but by high noon it'll disappear and the heat will be 95 degrees at the least. Well, that's Valia Springs for you; blistering in the summer, frigid in the winter. There's no in-between when you live in a valley in the mountains of northeastern Georgia.

"It's a good thing both the Catholic and public high schools let out for summer vacation on the same day. It was annoying how last year they kept the public school kids in two weeks longer than usual," Arthur comments.

My eyes shift between him and Frankie, and I can't help but notice how different they are. The two of them are pretty much polar opposites; after seven years of knowing them I *still* have no idea how the two of them ended up being best friends. Arthur's book-smart and a bona fide genius, while Frankie's street-smart and pretty average in the academic world. Arthur's as Polish as you can get, and Frankie's as Italian as you can get. Arthur's super lanky, pale, and somewhat awkward, has dark blond hair and green eyes, and has to wear a GIANT pair of glasses, whereas Frankie is tall, tan, muscular, has wavy dark brown hair and brown eyes, and is literally the most handsome boy in my age group. So you can see why people might be curious as to how these two boys are nearly inseparable.

We reach the top of the hill just in time to hear cheers erupting from below us. It's the rest of our teammates, gathered in the outfield of the old baseball diamond, who've probably been waiting for the three of us for quite a while (hey, it's not *my* fault my mother "accidentally" threw away my mitt this morning and we had to go digging through the trash cans to find it!).

"Hey guys. Sorry to keep you waiting, but *the girl* needed help looking for something," Frankie jokes when we get down into the weed-filled, unkempt outfield. I roll my eyes at him. The others tease me about it, trying to be funny. I'm so used to the teasing I get that it doesn't bother me anymore.

"I swear Charlotte, you look more like a girl every year," Jack O'Grady, a carrot-haired, freckle-faced Irish kid declares out of the blue. I blush. None of the guys *ever* call me Charlotte. It just isn't natural; I've been known as Charley every summer since I came to Valia Springs seven years ago. There's an awkward silence, on account of no one likes talking about me being a girl and all, especially since both the public and Catholic school ninth graders had to watch a movie about 'the wonders of puberty and maturation' and all the other crap no normal person likes to talk about. It doesn't help the fact that I'm a little over developed. Having an ideal body shape isn't all it's cracked up to be, though. Sometimes I feel odd because most of the other girls aren't as curvy as me.

The awkward silence is finally broken by JC, a short but overly confident tough kid with a lot of spunk, who complains loudly, "Are we gonna play baseball, or what?" And with that, we run to our positions.

Larry St. Joseph goes over to first base, followed by Jack at second. Danny Edwards takes shortstop, leaving me at third. Juan Carlos "JC" Ramirez is pitcher (Frankie's usual position, except for when he's batting, which he happens to be getting ready to do in a few moments) or any other position that's unoccupied while its usual player is batting, Mickey Johnson takes left field and, finally, Max Finkle is in center. No one ever plays right field, except when I'm batting, cuz I happen to be the only lefty on the team. In that case, Mickey and Max just shift to the right.

Everyone on the field backs up, *way* up, because there's no question to how far Frankie can hit. On many an occasion he's hit the ball over the hill, which in our opinion is like a pro knocking it outta the park. So it shouldn't be surprising that at the age of fifteen Frankie already played on both the Catholic and public high school varsity baseball teams this past spring (as a *starter*). Their seasons ended a week or so ago, so he'll play with our team the rest of the summer, which I suppose suits him just fine; he eats, sleeps, and breathes baseball, there ain't no doubt about that. As I'm thinking all of this, someone from behind me yells, "Charley! Look out!" Before I can wrap my brain around the 'look out' part of the warning something sails through the air and hits me square in the chest. The wind is knocked out of me and I fall hard on my back, taking a second before I can suck in any breath. Gasping for air and writhing in pain, I feel really stupid for not paying attention; but hey, on the bright side, the ball somehow landed in my glove. I just got Frankie Deluccio out.

⤳

Luckily my chest isn't sore anymore, thank God, but I had to sit out for a while; I even thought I was gonna start tearing up there for a second because the pain was so intense, but luckily I kept myself from crying. Boys really lose respect for you if you cry in front of them, so I've worked hard to make sure they've never caught me in the act.

I pull my shoulder length, medium brown hair into a short ponytail as we all sit down at the counter in our favorite diner, *Dee-Dee's*. It's probably about 2:30, we've been playing non-stop baseball for hours, and finally we're so hungry we couldn't stand it anymore, so we headed on over to the cute little eatery on Main Street. Penny Honeyduke, our favorite waitress (not to mention the prettiest girl in town and older sister of *the* Heather Honeyduke. Heather's the uncontested leader of the popular group of girls at my school who idiotically call themselves 'The Pretty Posse'), comes over to take our orders.

"The usual, please," Max says to Penny, and within a few moments nine bottles of Coca-Cola are lined up on the counter. Max, who's paying, pulls out a dollar. Cokes are only ten cents, but we always give Penny the full dollar, ten cents extra as a tip.

I look down at my pale hands. I think about my skin a lot, and I know I shouldn't, but it irritates me how I get sunburned so easily. It can be really embarrassing, especially because my shoulders and face get sunburned the worst. And I'm short. I'm slightly over five-foot-one and I have a feeling I'm not going to grow much more than that. I'll be lucky if I get to five-foot-two. And don't even get me started on my eyes. They aren't even a color, they're like some dull gray color and the only time they look different is when I'm crying; then it's like the tears stain my eyes a vibrant blue. I guess to sum it up I'm a very plain and simple-looking girl, but I'm not ugly. You'd think I am by my description, but I guess my "confidence and inner-beauty shine through like a rose in a glass vase," as my mother likes to tell me. The other thing she tells me is that "makeup would enhance my already beautiful looks and make them even more noticeable," but that's where I put my foot down. There is no way in Heaven or Hell that I will ever wear makeup. It's too girly and I refuse. Same thing with jewelry. My mother wants me to get my ears pierced, or at least wear a simple bracelet or necklace, but I just will not do it. I swear my mother wishes I wasn't so boyish; she wishes I was just like Heather Honeyduke and her sycophants. That's why I like to remind her every Sunday that she's lucky enough she can get me to wear the uniform skirt for my school and a dress for Church and the social dinners on Sunday nights. If you ask me, I think my mother should just take Heather and adopt her. Then I could switch lives with her and have Penny as an older sister instead of being an only child.

"Why Charlotte Marie Mason, how are you on this beautiful first day of summer?" Penny asks me in her sweet Southern drawl.

"Mighty fine, thank you Miss Penny," I smile at her. She would be such a great sister. If only, if only...

"I heard your mother's hosting the Catholic Women's Society Supper this Sunday evening –" Penny starts, when JC rudely snorts and shoots soda out of his nose. He thinks it's so hilarious I actually have to attend those sorts of things, and he thinks it's even more incredulous that I (even forcibly) wear a dress. "She's the best cook in the whole West Side of town. So when you go home, you just tell her that," Penny says without missing a beat; she acts as though JC *didn't* just laugh at such an important social gathering. To her family and all the other East Side girls, going to the Catholic Women's Society dinners is an important rite of passage from girl to womanhood. In the words of Larry, I'd rather they "gag me with a spoon."

Well, we're all enjoying ourselves and drinking ice-cold Coke and laughing at inside jokes when Tom, a waiter (and not to mention yet *another* boy in this world after Penny's heart), goes over to a big radio and tunes into the baseball station. Right now the Yankees are playing away at the White Sox, and are up by three.

Frankie and I are H-U-G-E Yankees fans (hence my untouchable, permanently-on-my-head Yankees baseball cap that my grandpa gave me), and my granddad even played for them for a few years (at the same time as Babe Ruth!). As long as I've known Frankie it's been our dream to one day play for the Yankees. I know I'm a long shot, but I suppose I'll just use my secret weapon: *nepotism*. Frankie's gonna make it on talent alone, no doubt about that. Arthur figures he'll try for the Yanks, too, but he's just too much of (and I love him like a brother when I say this) an egghead. He's younger than I am by about three months and yet he's two grades ahead of everyone on the team. The really ironic thing is that every single one of my teammates goes to the public school, whereas I must go to St. Maria Goretti Catholic High School. It's really frustrating at times because I have no friends at my school. There used to be this girl named Shirley, and we were pretty close friends, but she moved when I was in seventh grade. Everyone at my school thinks I'm weird, nobody wants to be my friend, and every day I either have the Pretty Posse or Biff Richardson and his cronies pointing out my every mistake and flaw. I'm not trying to get your sympathy or anything; everything I have to endure during the school year is something that will make me stronger. And as the old phrase goes, "This too shall pass." Anyway, everyday during the school year I walk with Frankie and Arthur to their school, then I just cross the road, pass the church, and I'm standing in front of the Hell I must deal with five days a week for nine months of the year. I begged my parents to let me go to the public high school, but they wouldn't let me. They explained they wanted me to have a strong Catholic education and that I should be thankful my parents can afford tuition at such an expensive school. When I walk home with Arthur and Frankie I have to meet them behind their school's dumpsters because every time they try to come to *my* school to meet me the girls at my school either stop whatever they're doing, stare, whisper to their friends, snicker, or gape at us. To put it bluntly, it's really annoying. But the walk to and from school with my best friends makes my day brighter. They always make me laugh and smile when I'm really down about something; I'm always happy when I'm with them. They remind me there's only three more years and then all three of us are out of here leaving this town and chasing our dreams in the most amazing city in America. *Just three more years.*

I'm brought back to the present when everyone in the diner starts cheering.

"What just happened?" I ask Frankie, "I wasn't paying attention." Frankie gives me an incredulous look, then smiles and replies, "The Yankees just got a double. Where've you been?" I don't have a chance to respond because at that moment everyone in the diner groans. I tap Arthur on the shoulder and when he turns around I ask him what just happened now, because neither Frankie nor I knew what the groan was for.

"The man on second tried to steal third but was tagged out," he responds.

The rest of the afternoon is a beautiful blur of the baseball game, chilled Coca-Cola, the smiles that come with a game well played, the sweltering heat of a summer afternoon, and the nearly tangible friendship the guys and I share as we walk home that evening. It's been a great first day of summer, no complaints here. We heard on the radio that it's gonna be a scorcher tomorrow, so after much persuasiveness we convince Frankie that we should go to The Pond instead of playing baseball. We walk home and once we reach the corner, five kids go down Thomas Lane and the rest of us (me, Arthur, Larry and Frankie) head down Wilson Street. Larry's house is right on the corner, Arthur lives three doors up on the left, and me and Frankie are the last two houses on the street, across from each other, his on the right side and mine on the left.

Our houses are mirror images of each other, both inside and out. The main difference is that his house is painted a pale blue and my house is a faint yellow. Our bedrooms are opposite each other and our windows face each other, which makes late night flashlight Morse Code conversations just that much easier. We both have trellises on the side of our houses leading up to our bedroom window. Sometimes on late summer nights, when the sky is perfect and our parents are in a good enough mood to let us, we meet up to take a midnight walk through the field beyond our houses. It's always peaceful and quiet, a perfect time to stargaze into the velvety black sky dotted with millions of crystals that make up the Milky Way. The warm summer night's breeze ripples the tall grass and makes a small brushing sound that echoes throughout the valley. In the distance the Appalachian Mountains loom like giant gray ghosts cast in the silvery glow of the midnight moon. They wrap around our little valley like a scarf, and the hollers that seem close in the daytime seem like a lifetime away in the dark. We become engulfed by the thousands of fireflies that dance around in the steamy mist that radiates off the ground because of the humidity. Those are the beautiful midsummer nights in Valia Springs I will never forget.

Frankie and I reach the dead end of our street and turn onto the walkways leading up to the front steps of the front porch of our houses. We wave good bye to each other as we simultaneously disappear into the doorways of our homes.

"Hello! I'm home," I call into the foyer. The house is cool from all of the fans we have on, causing the sweet smell of the kitchen to circulate throughout the first floor. Music is playing softly from the radio in the living room. It's a country song, which is normal for my house. Almost everyone in town listens to the soulful, heartfelt crooning of the country singers. It drifts through open windows all the time in the summer; it's almost as if it were the town's theme music.

"We're in the dining room, honey," Mother replies in her sing-song voice. I walk in and sit down at the table just as Mother sets a bowl of mashed potatoes next to my plate. She sits down next to my father and I help myself to her delicious cooking. Dinner is excellent as usual, but there's an odd silence I just can't seem to shake off. Ginger, our old Dachshund, licks my ankle under the table. Father clears his throat.

"Your mother and I have some exciting news," he says placidly. I look from him to Mother and then back.

"Well, what is it, then?" I ask somewhat impatiently after a dramatic silence.

"We're moving on August first." Mother says it. She looks down at her plate solemnly and waits for me to reply.

"To somewhere close by, right?" my voice raises slightly as I wait hopefully for a good answer. Mother shakes her head slowly.

"We're moving in with your grandparents in New York," Father says quietly, and I know he's dead serious. My heart seems to stop. I'm suddenly not hungry anymore. I can feel my throat tighten and my eyes moisten. I'm happy to be with my grandparents, but I don't want to move away. I can't just leave behind my best friends in the world!

"Pumpkin, let us explain..." my mother begins.

"No!" I say much louder than I intend to. I stand up quickly, knocking my fork to the floor, and storm up to my room before they can see me crying. I slam the door and the tears come faster than you can say 'last summer'. I crash onto my bed, cover my face with my pillow, and cry myself to sleep.

CHAPTER 2

The Pond

I wake up to a thick ray of sunlight filtering through the window and right into my face. My eyes are red and puffy, not to mention filled with all that gross crusty stuff in the corners of them. It's probably from all the crying I did last night. Suddenly, there's a tap on my window. Not made by a hand, but like a pebble or something. It happens again, and again. I'm starting to get really annoyed so I go over to my window, slide it open, and holler irritably, "CUT IT OUT!!!" I'm about to slam my window closed when eight familiar voices call, "Charley! Get down here! It's almost nine thirty!" I look down and there's the whole team, right below my window, staring up at me in the clothes I wore yesterday but forgot to take off before going to sleep, and my eyes are like the kind space aliens are supposed to have.

"Well, don't just stand there, HURRY UP!" JC yells at me, and I know I can't keep them waiting any longer or risk a riot. Boys can be so impatient sometimes.

I grab some clean clothes, run into the bathroom, close the door, lock it, strip down, as fast as possible put on my bathing suit and a clean pair of clothes on top of it, brush my teeth and wash my eyes out in less than two minutes (if that's humanly possible), hop every two steps down the stairs, race to the kitchen, grab a thermos filled with sweet ice tea, slide into my sneakers, snatch a towel from the linens closet, and as I'm jogging out the door and down the front steps I slap my Yankees cap on tight.

"Jeez, Charley, what took ya so long?" Max laughs.

"Someone must not have got enough of her beauty sleep," Mickey jokes.

"I'm sorry guys. I had a real rough night. I'll tell ya about it when we get to the Pond," I explain to them. Most of the guys shrug like it really doesn't matter that they had to wait so long to go to the Pond. JC, of course, who's extremely impatient, is irritated with me and I'll be lucky if he talks to me at all this whole afternoon; he's just that kind of person.

We all head on over to the Pond, Larry reaching it quicker than anyone. He is the fastest of us all, he can outrun nearly all of the other high school kids, and he just loves running.

Anyway, we reach the edge of the woods, snake our way through the trees, which are green, mossy, and surrounded by ferns, and arrive at the clearing and the Pond. The ground is a mix of moist dirt and dry sand surrounding a small pond, only about the size of one and a half Olympic swimming pools. It's not very deep, maybe fifteen feet at the most, and filled with tall, slimy strands of seaweed that entwine your legs and creep up your torso like giant octopus tentacles. It's a man-made waterhole that originally was going to be the town's pool but it was too close to the town junkyard. So they just left the dug-up hole and filled it with spring water. That was probably twenty years ago. There's also a lone willow tree that resides at the water's edge and hangs out over the Pond. There's a branch that someone long ago tied a tire swing to, and we like to use it to swing and dive into the water. The boys and I are the only people who ever hang out at the Pond; everyone else thinks it's gross because the dump is right next to it. We don't go here frequently, but it's always nice because it's so private.

We're all wearing our bathing suits under our clothes, so we pull off our shirts, shorts, shoes, and socks and fling them on the sandy shore around us. My bathing suit is a navy blue one-piece that ties around my neck. I still get a little self-conscious now and then when I go swimming with the guys, because I don't like how I look in my tight swimsuit. It's not that I look bad; in fact it's the exact opposite outcome that concerns me. I've just always been extremely conservative.

I dive in, and the cool water replenishes my already slightly-burnt skin.

If there's one thing I do almost as good as baseball, it's swimming. I didn't know how 'til I moved here when I was seven. My first summer here was mostly spent learning how to swim. The reason why I had to learn how to swim is this: I wanted to join the boys' baseball team, so they took a majority vote to let me play. It was a tie (Frankie, Arthur, Jack and Max voted me on, while JC, Larry, Mickey and Danny wouldn't allow it) so it was decided that I had to prove myself worthy. I was challenged to A) play a game of baseball with them, and they would see if I was good enough, B) hold my breath underwater while swimming, totally immersed, the length of the Pond, and finally C) climb up the old willow tree and dive off the highest branch into the Pond below. This last feat ended up breaking my left arm when I slipped off the branch I was going to dive off of, fell hard onto the sandy shore directly around the tree trunk, and refused to let the boys see me cry or scream from the pain; I rolled off the bank into the water and hollered soundlessly beneath the surface. After breaking my arm *and not even crying about it* like normal girls, they let me join them (but not without a surprising amount of apologies). The victory would probably have been more meaningful had I not broken my throwing and batting arm; hence, I couldn't play baseball with them until the following summer.

I dive deep beneath the surface of the water, but only in the more shallow areas where the Pond floor is still smooth and sandy. I can't stand swimming too deep into the kelp. There's just something about it that makes you truly believe there are sea monsters living within it, lurking, just waiting for the moment when you become ensnared and escaping your watery grave is improbable. It's silly, I know, but that's just one part of the magic and mystery of the Pond. I like to think it's enchanted.

"Hey, what was it you was gonna tell us 'bout last night? I mean no offense Charley, but you didn't look too good when you opened your window this mornin'. You kinda –and don't take this too harsh- looked like an alien," Mickey says to me as I emerge from the depths of the water. I roll my eyes at him but pull myself up onto the warm sand and beckon everyone over to hear my story. Once everyone is gathered 'round, I take a deep breath, close my eyes, and enunciate each syllable of the following sentence: "I'm moving to upstate New York on August first." I don't open my eyes 'til the shouts and cries of protest and confusion cease. When I finally open them, though, I'm staring right into Frankie's eyes. We each hold our gaze there for a moment longer, and then I hastily look away after the gravitational pull vanishes.

"Well, at least we'll have time to celebrate your 15th birthday with you," Frankie says quietly.

"This is SO unfair," Danny exclaims.

"In that case, we gotta make this summer real special," Arthur declares.

"But first, let's eat. I'm STARVING!" Max hollers. Well, we can't ignore Max's ever-present hunger pains, so we have a somewhat picnic brunch under the willow tree. We pass out peanut butter and jelly sandwiches to everyone and sit in a row, silently enjoying all the lip-smacking goodness of a classic American sandwich.

"Dammit! I dropped my sandwich in the dirt!" JC yelps. I sigh. I'm so used to the boys swearing around me, but it still kinda bothers me. Frankie swears in Italian so I don't know what he's saying, but by far JC swears the most. I've even swore on occasion, but that's another story.

"Nice goin'," Larry says exasperatedly as he rips off half of his sandwich and gives it to JC.

"Aww, forget it, I ain't hungry anyway," JC replies snidely. He hops onto the tire swing and flings himself into the Pond, splashing and drenching me, Arthur, and Frankie. Arthur looks annoyed, but I and Frankie laugh. We jump in the water and start a splashing fight with JC. Soon, everyone's joined us. It's a heck of a lotta fun, considering the temperature is well over a 100 and getting hotter.

"Hey! Does anyone wanna race me from one side of the pond to the other?" I ask, my competitiveness getting the best of me.

"Sure," Frankie shrugs.

"I'll be on the other side of the pond to judge who the winner is," Arthur declares. All the boys get out of the water to wait eagerly at the finish line. I line up parallel to Frankie.

"On your mark…get set…GO!" the boys cheer in unison. We both take off swimming pretty fast and steady. I'm attempting to beat Frankie, but that's not gonna happen, considering I'm not nearly as strong as he is (but for a girl I'm pretty strong). Toward the middle of the pond I'm starting to get tired, and my arms are starting to ache really bad. Frankie, who was once way ahead of me, has slowed down and dropped back to where I am.

"You don't have to let me win just cuz I'm a girl and it's the polite thing to do," I say to him as I flip over to do the backstroke.

"I ain't lettin' ya win, I'm just savin' my energy for when we get real close to the finish; then I'll put on a burst of speed and beat you," he explains.

"Well have a nice time with that," I laugh as I flip back onto my stomach and speed off. *Ha, I'm almost there,* I think, *he can't beat me now.* But as I turn my head to the side to take a breath I see him quickly catching up to me. There's only two yards left!

I swim as fast as possible, not bothering to see if he's beating me, and drag myself up to the shore once I reach it, panting.

"Tie!" Arthur calls, and his voice echoes and bounces off the trees in the clearing. The whole team cheers us both, not wanting to choose sides. Frankie, who is standing, offers me his hand and pulls me to my feet.

"Nice race, kid," he grins genuinely. "You were some real competition, as usual."

The thing about Frankie is that he's very polite to girls, but this can be a problem; he wants to be a gentleman to me as much as possible, although he knows I want to be treated as his equal, but of course he would be humiliated if he ever got beat by a girl (which, of course, he never has).

We're pretty beat from all the swimming we've been doing today, so we all go back to where our stuff is and relax on the sand. Before we know it, it's late afternoon. We're all lying on our towels, basking in the intense glow of the afternoon sun, when a faint trace of cigarette smoke makes its way through the clearing. It's strange to be smelling the smoke, considering no one ever goes into the woods. I'm as curious as ever about why we can smell the mysterious scent, and by the way the boys are looking around questioningly, I can tell they're curious, too. I call out, "Where is that coming from?" To which Arthur replies, "It seems to be emanating from the junkyard. We'd better go take a look."

One by one, we all follow Frankie around the barbed wire fence to where the smoke is strongest. As we approach the junkyard gates, we are surprised to find them unlocked and partially open. As I peer through the haze that's gathering around the entrance, I spot several young men and motorcycles a few yards away. It's an immediate shock; Greasers, as the stereotype is known to be, is a form of gangster/ne'er-do-well that is neither tolerated by civilians nor the law enforcers in this town. The Catholic Women's Society spent all of last summer publicizing the evils of Greasers and their way of life, fully assuming that their voices were heard loud and clear; in fact, this actually provoked some of our town's adolescent boys to become closet Greasers as a form of rebelliousness. With every passing minute, though, it became evident that these young men were more interested in wearing leather, slicking back their hair with hair gel, polishing their motorcycles, and smoking cigarettes than disturbing us. It's a funny thing, though. Motorcycles were banned from Valia Springs because they're associated with Greasers, and I've never even heard the engines revving on these bikes. Also, how in the world did they get cigarettes? It's nearly punishable by law in this town to smoke under the age of 21. The fact of the matter is that these guys are East-siders. There's only maybe five of them, but they're the low-down mean creeps of the East side. I know for a fact that one of them is Biff Richardson's older brother, Rocky. He's like 18 or something.

It takes me a minute before I realize one of the Greasers is staring right at me...well, not my face, but somewhere slightly south of it. Of course I just have to be wearing my obnoxiously tight bathing suit. I gulp. A chill runs down my spine and goosebumps spread up my arms. *Oh, Lord.*

Frankie's realized this too, so he instinctively moves in front of me, blocking my body from the guy's view. Their eyes lock for a few minutes. Frankie's jaw is set, and though I can't see the front of his face I can just picture the intense glare on it. I don't know why, but I'm holding my breath. I finally release the pressure in my lungs when Frankie slowly turns to me and says calmly, "Go back to the Pond and put your clothes on, please." I jog back to the clearing and, as quickly as possible, pull on my T-shirt, shorts, socks, sneakers, and last but not least, my Yankees cap. When I turn to walk back to the dump, the team is already arriving, single file, onto the beach. "Let's go, guys," Frankie calls, and everyone grabs their stuff and starts heading through the trees towards the road. Arthur, Frankie and I walk out to the road last, not saying anything, but realizing the awkward silence between us isn't meant to be broken. We walk together, hands in our pockets and heads down. It's strange how such a tragic night can lead to a beautiful day, and then by afternoon turn into a somewhat creepy situation, only for me to come out physically unscathed. It really makes you think about the weird and yet wonderful world God created for us. At least when I get home there will be pork chops on the table and a bed with fresh sheets. Those things, I hope, never change.

CHAPTER 3

Sunday Night Supper

"**C**harlotte, get down here right now and help me greet our guests," Mother shouts irritably up the stairs.

"I'll be down in a jiffy," I call down to her. I glance at myself in the mirror once more before turning toward the door and trudging my way down the hallway and stairs to the foyer. I grumpily mumble about my stupid pastel pink dress. It has a ribbon with a bow in the front that goes around my waist, and the knee-length skirt portion of it fluffs and poufs out. The whole thing has a layer of light pink lace on top. It's simply *dreadful*.

The doorbell rings just then. I open it and force a smile. It's Mrs. Honeyduke and the other moms from the Catholic Women's Society (otherwise known as the 'CWS'), who've all arrived together precisely at six o'clock.

"Good evening Charlotte," they say to me as I hold the door open for them and they make their way to the dining room. They're wearing their fanciest dresses tonight, like every other Sunday night. Penny walks through the door and smiles warmly at me.

"You can sit next to me at dinner if you'd like," she tells me. I nod thankfully. I'll at least have *someone* to talk to.

Next, the Pretty Posse struts in, one after the other, their noses stuck up in the air as if they smelled something foul. None of them bother to so much as glance my way; they just walk right past me and briskly stride to the dining room. They're all wearing the same dress as I am, only in different pastels. Anne is wearing pastel blue, Sarah is wearing pastel green, Ella's dress is lilac, Sophie's dress is pastel orange, Catherine's dress is pastel yellow, Mary's dress is white, and 'Queen' Heather's dress is the exact same one I have. This caused much drama at our Initiation Supper, when she shrieked in outrage at the sight of me, then ran to the bathroom and wouldn't stop crying hysterically until I came and apologized for embarrassing her in front of the whole Society. I begged my mother to let me get a new dress, but the department store in town had run out of dresses in my size. So I was forced to keep the dress. It is a constant reminder of Heather and her hatred towards me. I think she hates me so much on account of the day we moved to Valia Springs, she and her mother and the other women in the Catholic Women's Society came over to welcome us to the town (apparently they are the Official Welcoming Committee). Well,

Mrs. Honeyduke told Heather to introduce me to the other little girls in the town, but Heather didn't know where I was. She finally asked my mother, who replied that I had gone with a little boy into the backyard of the house across the street. Realizing what boy this was, she rushed over to the open gate leading into his backyard, and there I was, playing catch with *her* Frankie. As far as she was concerned, no bratty-good-for-nothing-new-girl-in-town was gonna steal the man she was sure to marry someday. *I* was the enemy; *I* was the only female in town standing in her way of being with him for the rest of her life. And there was no way in Heaven or Hell that Heather Honeyduke was gonna let some ugly tomboy ruin her chances. The only way to get rid of the possibility that Frankie might 'have a thing' for anyone other than herself was to squash that competition, and squash it *fast*. She would never admit it, but she considered me a threat the first time she met me. That is why on the first day of third grade, she spilled water on me at lunch and told everyone I'd "had an accident". She convinced her worshippers to spread rumors that I said mean stuff about others behind their back and a whole bunch of other awful, untrue things that is sure to get people to hate me. Her logic was based on the fact that no boy ever liked an 'unpopular'. But when she realized Frankie (along with Arthur, but he wasn't taken into her account) and I walked to and from school, she knew that desperate times called for desperate measures. Soon she and her apostles were calling me ugly, stupid, a loser, and all sorts of other profanities that her jealousy made her say. And when I got the same dress as her for the CWS dinners, that was the last straw. She got that dress so she could be the most gorgeous girl in our whole age group, only to find that *I* of all people was standing in her way once again, wearing *her* beautiful dress. Mind you, I hate 'our' dress and don't find it attractive at all. She managed to use this for her advantage, though. Now she can't stop whispering (just loudly enough for me and her clones to hear) about how she looks so much better than I do. After all of these years of putting up with her, I've come to realize I don't give a dime about what she thinks of me. I only care about what my grandparents and best friends think about me. Everything mean she says just kind of gets disintegrated by my shield of self-confidence. Really, though, I don't hate her at all; in fact, I truly feel sorry for her. And even if she's mean to me a lot, it's easy for me to forgive her. Weird, right?

I go into the dining room and grab a seat at the table next to Penny. Ginger is snoozing under my seat. The lacey drapes hung over the window are parted slightly in the middle, and a ray of orange-yellow sunset beams across the room and illuminates in a perfect spot on the cream-colored wall. It barely grazes the top of Penny's head, turning her strawberry blonde hair into pure gold.

"So, Penny," Mrs. Anderson asks from the other side of the table, "have you heard anything from Ricardo?" It's an innocent enough question, but I can tell by the way her eyes mist over that Penny's answer is like a nail in her heart: "I haven't heard a word for months."

Ricardo (who everyone calls Ricky) is Frankie's older brother and Penny's sweetheart. A little over a year ago, after they graduated from high school, he got an acceptance letter to Notre Dame. Right before he left he proposed to Penny, and they promised each other that as soon as he gets back home they'll get married. He originally kept in touch and sent a letter or called her every week. Now, though, he apparently hasn't made contact with anyone since April. Penny's worried that some pretty college girl has caught his attention and Ricky is just too nice to break her heart through a letter or phone call. She really has nothing to worry about, though, because Ricky is so in love with her it sometimes makes me want to puke. Just seeing them together all the time, holding hands, sending each other love letters, going to dances together, going on dates, and just plain looking at each other, makes me believe true love does exist.

Ricky and Frankie look a lot alike, except for the maturity difference (of which there is little), and they both resemble their father. Their mother, on the other hand, died the year before I moved here. I'm told that she was beautiful, she was a member of the CWS, and she was the best seamstress in town. I wish I could've met her, she sounded very nice. I've only seen a picture of her face, which is displayed in her brother's restaurant, *Salvatore Anetrini's*. It's the best eatery in town, and as you can imagine, it specializes in Italian food. Frankie's dad works part time there; he owns and runs Deluccio's Garage, the local mechanics place. Apparently, Frankie and Ricky went to the Catholic school until their mother died; afterward, their dad couldn't afford to send them there without the extra income from their mom's various sewing jobs.

Suddenly, my mother stands up to say the blessing.

"Dear Lord, we thank you for another beautiful week in our valley. You have brought prosperity to our husbands and peace in the household. Thank you for this meal that we share in your name. Amen."

"Amen," everyone says in unison, and we raise our glasses in a toast. The women are drinking white wine, while we younger girls must drink grape juice. Mother comes around and serves us our food, the traditional chicken, green beans, salad, roll, and mashed potatoes with gravy. Gossip breaks out all over the long table, slowly at first (as people are eating), but then what once was a low rumble now becomes an epidemic of rumor-spreading, secret-spilling, and reports from eavesdroppers and spying neighbors. These ladies can be ten times worse than the girls in my school, and that's bad enough in itself. I've been eating for two minutes and already I've heard about Mrs. Baker's secret rhubarb pie recipe losing (for the first time in nine years) the county's pie contest, Mr. Johnson "had some gastro-intestinal distress" in the barber shop last Thursday, Harriet (a waitress at Dee-Dee's) spilled split-pea soup all over old Mrs. Nickles, and apparently J.C. was spotted smoking a cigarette behind the dumpster in back of his father's butcher shop.

As far as I'm concerned, gossip is gross. All is does is make other people feel bad when you talk about them behind their back, not to mention half the stuff gossip consists of is either a bold-faced lie or greatly embellished. That's another one of the reasons I'll never be popular: literally *all* of the women and girls I know (with the exception of my grandma and Penny) treat gossiping like it's an Olympic sport. And gossip is just another reason why these Catholic Women's Society Sunday Night Suppers are so awkward; because I choose to remain silent, despite my usually outgoing and talkative personality. This fact, though, makes me an outsider within the Society. In the first couple of gatherings I went to all of the women were friendly to me because I am Judy's daughter (and they were probably thinking, 'Well, if she's anything like her mother she'll be invaluable to this Society') but it seems they caught on to my sullen attitude quickly. Originally, after they realized I didn't participate, they just whispered about me and spread rumors about how I must be mute or deaf or both, but now they just ignore me. I'm the black sheep of the whole group, I realize, because apparently I was supposed to grow out of being 'one of the boys' by now (it was assumed to be a passing phase) and, obviously, I didn't. And this brings me back to the reasons why my mother and I don't get along, because she is always trying to take my baseball dreams and nip them in the bud. The only reason I'm still allowed (somewhat) to be 'one of the boys' is because my usually quiet father finally stood up for me, which ended up being a huge yelling match between my parents. They settled on a compromise, of which I must go to/do anything my mother wishes (with a few exceptions, i.e. the makeup and jewelry issue) as long as she doesn't interfere with my baseball and/or friends.

My father used to be a lot like me, my mother claims, until he came back from Germany. She says something died in him, made his soul silence to the world around it, because of the war. I wouldn't remember the 'old dad' because I was just a baby then. Maybe it's better this way, though; that way I don't miss what he used to be. When Father's off at work and I get home from school early I'll sneak upstairs to start my homework...and sometimes I'll hear my mother weeping soundlessly in her bedroom. I know that she only cries about two things: the miscarriage of my baby sister, and my father's apparent absentness. He reminds me of John Wayne in *The Quiet Man*, one of my all-time favorite movies. In a bunch of ways, my father and Frankie's father are alike; they both seem lost in their own realms, with a constant look of distance on their faces and deep worry lines that crease on their brow. It's as if their silence speaks louder than any word they've ever uttered. But sometimes, on a rare occasion, my father will take the portable radio and a lawn chair and go sit in a somewhat hidden, shady place behind the garage and listen to anything, be it news, music, or sports. I'll creep slyly through the tight gap between the garage and fence until I round the corner and sit next to him. He acts as if he doesn't notice me, but eventually in our little time together he'll take me by the hand. I'll barely notice it 'til it's gone. The sweetest memory of all of these times, though, was once two summers ago, when some big band swing from the early 40's came on the radio. He pulled me to my feet and we danced to it. I could see the shadow of a smile form on his face as we twirled around. It was the first glimpse I'd seen of the man my mother used to know. After the song ended, he sat back down immediately; it was like I'd dreamt the whole thing. Other times he'll ask me questions about me and my life. I expect him to not really pay attention, considering while I'm talking he'll just stare off into space, but something about his thoughtful expression and occasional nod adds suspicion that he really does care what I think and say.

My reverie is yanked out from under me when suddenly there's a sharp knock on the partially open dining room door. My father widens the space to reveal. his head, neck, and shoulders.

"I beg your pardon, ladies, but I would be grateful if you would kindly excuse Charlotte for a moment. She has a…a visitor in the foyer," he announces in his quiet, exhausted voice. I get out of my chair and make my way to the door, but not in time to block Heather's view of the foyer, where she spies Frankie with his hands in his pockets and leaning against the wall. Her face darkens to the most hateful glower I've seen her spew at me in quite a while. I shut the door behind me, though, so she doesn't get the privilege of gazing at him in that way that she always does at church and around town. It's somewhat of an intense gaze, too, which makes it all the more obsessive.

"Hey Charley," he smiles at me, and then gives me the ole once-over (sometimes it's still difficult for the guys to see me in my dress).

"What's up?"

"I just figured I'd return your bat to ya. Thanks for lettin' me borrow it this afternoon." He hands me my bat. He never uses his regular bat (also known as his 'lucky' bat) for plain old practice, only for games; that way, he reasons, it'll never run outta luck.

"No problem," I shrug at him.

"Well, I better not keep ya too long, or those ladies'll get impatient. On second thought, you don't wanna be in there anyway," he laughs to himself.

"I'd love to hang out longer, but my mother's gonna kill me if I'm not in there in two seconds," I sigh wistfully.

"Sorry. Well, I'll talk to ya later. Flashlight me as soon as you go to bed, OK?" and with that, he turns and walks out the door.

I streak up the stairs and into my room like a bolt of lightning, throw the bat on my bed and race back downstairs and into the dining room. I've just barely sat down when a very unpleasant yet faint *squish* reverberates from the seat of my chair. The part of my dress that I'm sitting on slides in the chair a little and feels slimy and wet. At first my mind is cringing, *Oh, Ginger, what did you do this time?!* But then I notice Heather, who's trying her hardest to look innocently away from the crime scene. A slight smile that she's trying to hide appears for a millisecond. My heart sinks.

"Would you all please excuse me? I need to use the lavatory," I say gently to the women around me, and back away from the table and out the door, making sure my hind quarters are free of everyone's view. After I shut the door I dash down the hall into the bathroom, close and lock the door, and turn to look at the back of my dress in the floor-length mirror. Just as I feared, there is a distinct brown splotch on the rear of my dress. Judging by the smell and texture of it, I identify it as gravy. Well, isn't that just peachy-keen?

So I take off my dress, and, in my petticoat, camisole and bloomers (yes, I am forced to actually wear those), I begin to scrub the stain rigorously with a few sheets of damp toilet tissue and some baking soda.

"Honey, are you alright in there? You've been gone for a while and I was beginning to get worried," Mother calls from the other side of the door. "What's wrong, dear?"

"Everything's fine, Mother. It's just that I got some gravy on my dress and it's not washing out," I reply impatiently.

"Well, if you'll please unlock the door I will help you," she tells me in a way that means I *have* to unlock it even if I don't want to. So I do. But as soon as she waltzes in and takes one glance at the stain, she nearly faints into the bathtub.

"Good Heavens! What on Earth did you *do* to that dress!?" she exclaims so loudly that people in Canada could hear her. An unshakeable awkward silence falls in the dining room directly after, and I can't help but picture Heather silently smirking to herself.

"Mother, I can explain-," I start, but she cuts me off.

"Charlotte, this is the *last straw*. I know you don't like these suppers, and I know you don't like the CWS, and I *certainly* know you hate this beautiful dress. But in all my years I've never met a young woman with such boldness to the extent of purposely ruining such an expensive article of clothing! You are grounded for the rest of the night, young lady, no ifs, ands, or buts about it!" Then she promptly smacks me on the butt, and it is mighty painful. As she pulls me by the ear out of the bathroom, down the hall, and past the living room, she watches me climb the stairs before turning to my father. He's sitting in his La-Z-Boy, his face impassible and absent as usual. She points an angry finger at him, ready to henpeck.

"And *you*," she's fuming so badly now, her voice has lowered to a quivering growl, "you couldn't have even come to help me! Did you see what she did? *Did you?* This is the most embarrassing moment of my life and you couldn't have even come to punish her for me! Why do I always have to look like the bad guy?! For all I care you can just sleep on the floor tonight, dammit!" She screeches this last sentence, throws my dirty dress at him as she slams the door with such force that it shakes the house.

I get into the safe haven that is my room just in time to peer out my window and watch everyone leave immediately, no questions asked. Somehow I know this incident will be all over town by tomorrow morning. As she exits my house and trots to her car, Heather takes one swift look up at me – and her eyes glisten as if to say, *Heather: 1, Charlotte: -2.*

Once night falls and I'm ready for bed, I pull out my flashlight and aim across the street into Frankie's window. The second summer here, Frankie was really interested in learning codes and secret languages. We practically spent the whole summer teaching each other how to use flashlights for Morse code conversations, but it was completely worth it. I spell out in Morse code: A-R-E_Y-O-U_A-W-A-K-E_

I soon get a reply: W-H-Y_D-I-D_E-V-E-R-Y-O-N-E_ L-E-A-V-E_E-A-R-L-Y_

I respond: M-Y_M-O-T-H-E-R_B-L-E-W_A_G-A-S-K-E-T_

He asks: W-H-Y_

I explain: B-E-C-A-U-S-E_H-E-A-T-H-E-R_P-U-T_ G-R-A-V-Y_O-N_M-Y_C-H-A-I-R_S-O_I-T_L-O-O-K-E-D_ L-I-K-E_I_H-A-D_A-N_A-C-C-I-D-E-N-T_W-H-E-N_I_ S-A-T_D-O-W-N_A-N-D_M-O-M_T-H-O-U-G-H-T_I_ S-T-A-I-N-E-D_M-Y_D-R-E-S-S_O-N_P-U-R-P-O-S-E_

Him: H-E-A-T-H-E-R_H-O-N-E-Y-D-U-K-E_

Me: T-H-E_O-N-E_A-N-D_O-N-L-Y

Him: A-R-E_Y-O-U_G-R-O-U-N-D-E-D

Me: W-H-A-T_D-O_Y-O-U_T-H-I-N-K

Him: I_W-I-L-L_T-A-K-E_T-H-A-T_A-S_A_Y-E-S_

We talk to each other for a little while longer, Until my mother pounds on my door angrily and yells that I need to quit the stupid conversation I was having because if the neighbors saw it, the light flashes would give them a seizure. I communicate this to Frankie and so we say our good nights and go to bed. I can't help but wonder how many more late-night-flashlight chats I have left, because from the way this summer is turning out, this could very well be my last one.

CHAPTER 4

Early in the Morning

M y eyes flutter open suddenly, and I roll onto my side to look at my bedside alarm clock, ticking away as usual. Blinking and rubbing my eyes, I find out that it is precisely 5:38 am. I yawn, sit up and stretch, wanting to sleep longer but realizing that I'm at the point where there's no going back into dreamland. So, I do what I always do: I put on some clothes and head out to my front porch to watch the sunrise over the mountains. It seems like I do this every morning after I've had a really bad fight with my mother.

I pad silently out of my room and down the stairs, trying to remain quiet as I slip out the front door. My parents don't really mind me sitting all by myself on the porch like this, and at least if they *do* mind, they never let on.

I sit sideways in our porch swing, my legs hanging off the edge of the right side of the swing and my head resting against a floral-print pillow on the left side. It's a little cool this morning, and it smells damp from the dew on the ground. It's a very similar smell to the earthy scent after a rainstorm, which is to me the best aroma in the whole world. It's fresh and clean and new, which is probably the best thing about mornings; they always fill you with hope that the day will be as good as the way it started. There are a few birds chirping from a tree on the side of my house that break the peaceful stillness and silence of the outdoors. I turn my head to stare across the street, and from behind Frankie's house I can see the crack of dawn starting to spread and glow.

I don't know how long I sit there, just staring at the approaching stream of light, when I hear the whisking sound of a bicycle scraping over the asphalt. I sit up and see none other than Frankie, riding down the street and chucking rolled up newspapers at the front doors of the other houses. I almost forgot he's the town's paper boy, although this is his last summer on the job. Twelve-year-old Jimmy Wells from two streets over is taking his job, not that Frankie minds.

Frankie's about to toss a newspaper on my porch when he skids to a stop and says jokingly, "Hey there, stranger." He gets off the bike, letting it carelessly drop to the ground, and comes up the walk to hand the newspaper to me.

"You done with your route already?" I ask tiredly.

"Yep. Just finished," he replies as I take the paper from him. He glances at his watch.

"What time is it?"

"Time for you to get a watch."

"Ha ha, very funny. Stick to your day job, Mr. Comedian," I roll my eyes.

"Sorry, I couldn't help myself," he smiles. "It's six o'clock, by the way."

"Oh. That means my parents will be getting up now." My stomach gurgles and rumbles loudly, bringing attention to the fact that I am quite hungry. "Hey, can you stay here for a second? I've got an idea…I'll be right back," I say as I get up and go into the house. Mother's clomping down the stairs in curlers, slippers and a bathrobe, looking as groggy as ever.

"Good morning, Mother," I fake cheeriness in my voice.

"Mornin'," she grunts.

"I've been thinking…why not let me make breakfast this morning?" I suggest, trying to suck up to her so my punishment for the dress incident last night won't be so severe. She pauses, eyeing me suspiciously, then shrugs.

"Go ahead," she sighs. She turns to go back up to her room to get dressed.

"Wait! Can Frankie help me?"

"Yes, fine," she replies absently before disappearing up the stairwell.

I jog back out to the porch.

"You wanna help me make breakfast?" I ask energetically.

"Uh...I guess..." I don't really give him a lot of time to answer before pulling him inside. There's like this brief spark that shoots up my arm as our hands touch. It's not exactly like an electric shock you get from touching a static-covered door knob. It's not painful and the tingling tremor goes all the way to my elbow before disappearing altogether.

I tug him down the hallway into the kitchen and flip on the lights.

"So what are we making?" he asks, sitting down at the little three-person table.

"Two words: French toast," I tell him as I go into the spices cabinet and pull out a shaker full of cinnamon. "Do you know how to make it?"

"Of course I do," he grins, "my Uncle Sal taught me...sorta." He gets up to come over to the spices cabinet, which is still open, and pulls out two random containers.

"Then why are you getting out the basil and oregano?" I laugh.

"Well, jeez, isn't that what you put in it?" he jokes as he puts the seasonings back.

"Here, let me help you," I fake-sigh exasperatedly. I get out four eggs from the refrigerator, some vanilla extract from the cupboard, and six slices of bread from the breadbox.

"I think I can take it from here," he tells me, but I still don't trust him, so I get the olive oil out of the pantry, put a thin layer in the pan, set it on the stove, and turn the burner on. Meanwhile, he's cracked the eggs in a bowl and is whisking them. Next he adds the cinnamon and vanilla and stirs vigorously. So vigorously, in fact, that it splashes all over the counter and onto his clothes. I giggle.

"I think I'll go back to my house to get changed now," he states as he bows deeply, and then grandly exits the kitchen.

I wait a few more moments until the oil sizzles and pops. Then I dip the bread in the egg mix and slap it into the pan. I do this with the rest of the bread, making sure to flip the bread in the pan so it's golden-brown and crispy on both sides. I serve the pieces on a tray once done, then place two pieces neatly on his plate and two on mine. I pour maple syrup over the French toast with a flourish, set the plates on the table, and lay the silverware out just as Frankie walks back in. The extra French toast is left in the pan with the heat low so my parents can have it in a few minutes.

"Allow me," Frankie says as he pulls my chair out for me. I sit down gracefully and act as if I'm sweeping a skirt out from under me as I sit.

In his best Italian accent, Frankie says, "Would you like milk to drink, Miss Mason?"

"*Sì, per favore*," I reply in Italian. He gets out two glasses and fills them with milk, then brings them over and sets them on the table. We're sitting across from each other at the table.

"Miss Mason, you are a marvelous chef," he tells me. "You should make breakfast for us every morning." He is still talking in a fancy accent. So I decide to join him and do my best British impression.

"Well, I *am* flattered you think so of my culinary skills. Tell me, how are things in the restaurant business?"

"My dear Uncle Salvatore has had an exceptional amount of customers as of late. The most popular dish on the menu appears to be the Eggplant Parmesan, although I prefer the veal and spaghetti."

"As do I, Mr. Deluccio. Now, I have an idea that I'd like your opinion on. At my upcoming birthday party, I was considering having a period of dancing in which all the guests can partake in. Do you think that would be a poor activity to have?"

"No, I dare say I do not think it is a horrid idea. Kindly elaborate on your suggestion."

"I've been pondering this idea for a while. I know my mother would greatly approve of classic ballroom dancing, but I've run into two predicaments: I can't dance whatsoever, and I don't have a dance partner."

"I beg your pardon, Miss Mason, but I believe I have a solution. I can teach you how to dance, and I shall be your escort to this grand occasion."

"How kind of you, Mr. Deluccio. Thank you so very much."

After we finish eating, my mother and father sit down and we serve them their food. They thank us, and knowing that they'd probably rather eat in privacy we go back out to the front yard. Frankie puts his bike back in his garage across the street and grabs his baseball gear. I grab my stuff, too, and we head on over to the field way before anyone else, getting in extra practice time before the rest of the team shows up.

CHAPTER 5

Dancing in the Rain

Hours later, it's a cloudy, gray, muggy afternoon at the baseball field. I'm up to bat, and Frankie's pitching. He doesn't say so, but I'm basically positive he's going easy on me. Both pitches were meatballs that I just happened to foul. He shakes his head to communicate to Arthur that no, he's not pitching a curve ball, then shakes his head again to indicate no, he's not pitching a change-up, either. He nods and I know that it's gonna be a fastball. So I swing as soon as he releases the ball and I make contact. The crack of the bat is thrilling, and as I run to first Larry tells me to keep going because apparently that ball went right over the hill. I just got my first home run! The guys don't even bother chasing after it. They'd rather let me relish the moment than try to get me out. I jog the bases, my hands in the air as I spin wildly and jump ecstatically in a crazy celebration dance, screaming for joy the whole way to home plate. When I tag the base everyone comes over to give me well-deserved pats on the back and plenty of cheers. I'm completely on Cloud 9.

The clouds are rolling in faster than you can say "thunderstorm" so we decide not to play one more inning, but it doesn't matter because we're leaving the field for the rest of the day anyway. Our tradition is that anyone on the team gets ice cream as a reward for their first homerun, and they get to keep the ball. As you can imagine, I'm filled with euphoria, smiling so hard my cheeks hurt. I thought this moment would never come! Suddenly Arthur interrupts the cheers.

"I got a real swell idea. Ya know how this is Charley's last summer?" he asks us. We all nod. "Well, why don't we give everybody a designated day to spend with her? We'll make a schedule of who gets Charley on what day. I even brought a sheet o' paper and a pencil to work on it now. By a show of hands, who thinks we should do this?" About three-quarters of our team agree. I'm pretty sure only JC and Max didn't raise their hands.

"OK, well that settles it," Arthur declares, "I'll get started on it. Frankie, do you wanna be first?" There's the slightest hint of a mischievous smile on Arthur's face.

"Put me down for last," Frankie replies flatly. An awkward silence follows where Frankie just frowns at Arthur. It is interrupted by Mickey, Max, and Larry. They've climbed onto the low-hanging dugout roof and are sitting on top of it in a row...spitting.

"Ha! I so beat you!" Mickey laughs. The boys are having a spitting contest.

"No you didn't! Mine's just in front of yours!" Larry argues.

"Oh, puh-leez. Watch this, amateurs," JC scoffs as he climbs up next to them. He hacks up a wad o' spit that sails onto the sidewalk about ten yards behind the dugout. No one else's saliva is even close. Jack and Danny climb up there, too, to take their turn with spitting. I decide to join them.

"Move outta the way, fellas. It's my turn," I claim as I push through them. When I spit, though, it lands only a few feet from where we are. It's really quite pathetic.

"Take another try," Jack tells me as he pats me on the back. I do, but it hits the ground only like three feet farther than the first glob. I feel pretty embarrassed, but the guys don't say anything about it. They just continue spitting until Arthur calls us over to check out the list. It reads:

1. Max Finkle------------------June 29th

2. Larry St. Joseph----------July 6th

3. Danny Edwards------------July 12th

4.   Jack O'Grady--------------July 15th

5.   Mickey Johnson-----------July 19th

6.   JC Ramirez----------------July 23rd

7.   Arthur Lyczkowski--------July 27th

8.   Francis Deluccio----------July 31st

Everyone tries to keep from cracking up as we read "Francis" Deluccio. The guys don't want to laugh at their fearless leader's name, but I'm pretty sure I and Arthur can get away with a few chuckles. Everyone else silences, though, when Frankie exclaims, "That's not even my real name!" That makes us laugh even harder, cuz we know his real name is just plain "Frank". Arthur and I have this huge inside joke about how we were at Frankie's house when we were little and his grandpa was over and called him Francis. Arthur and I burst out laughing and between fits of giggles we kept saying how Francis is a girl's name. We teased Frankie for weeks after that. It's still funny to think about.

"I'm sorry, Frankie. I couldn't help myself," Arthur apologizes in a very non-serious manner. I finally get my laughter under control. Frankie rolls his eyes at us and says, "Arthur, you are so immature." He doesn't say it in a mean way, just an 'I'm-kinda-annoyed-but-I'm-laughing-with-you-on-the-inside' way.

Suddenly we are all pelted with raindrops. The storm's finally arrived. Luckily, it's just rain, no thunder or lighting at all. But this is the kind of rainstorm that doesn't just have drops; it literally is like an endless waterfall.

"Arthur, take the guys to the ice cream shop and get some ice cream. Me 'n' Charley'll catch up with you in a little while," Frankie says. Arthur raises his eyebrows but does what he's told.

The boys make a mad dash across the road and into town. Frankie and I are all alone in the pouring rain. I look up at him.

"What are you up to?" I ask loudly so he can hear me over the wind and rain.

"I was gonna give you your first dance lesson," he smiles down at me. I hate being so much shorter than him. He puts both hands on my waist and I figure I'd better put my hands on his shoulders. This is something I've picked up from the movies I've seen.

"Now you step back with your right foot, then your left, then your right foot moves right, then your left foot moves right, then you step forward with your right foot, then step forward with your left foot. Got it?"

"Uh…kind of."

"Don't worry, just follow my lead." I try my best to remember what the heck I'm supposed to be doing. Everywhere I step, my foot squishes in the flooded infield dirt. I can barely see Frankie's face through the non-stop sheets of water. But I think I've actually caught on to this whole 'dancing' concept.

"You're doin' real good," Frankie tells me. I smile.

"Where'd you learn to dance?" I ask him.

"Ricky. He learned how to dance so he could take Penny to Prom. He taught me how to dance cuz he figured I'd need to know how someday."

"Have you heard anything from Ricky lately?"

"Um…" I can tell his face has fallen. I quickly change the subject.

"It's nice to just be alone for once. Ya know? Cuz it's just the two of us at the baseball diamond," I comment quietly.

"No kiddin'," Frankie agrees. He pulls me in closer and I stand on my toes to get to slightly lower than his eye level and put my arms around his neck and he leans down and I close my eyes-

BOOM! Thunder shakes the ground around us and startles me so I jump backwards. I avert my eyes and say (more to myself than to him), "The guys are waitin' for us. We better get going."

We walk in complete silence until we enter the ice cream parlor. I didn't entirely notice how drenched we are until we step inside and everyone is staring at us. I pull off my hat and take my hair out of its ponytail so it'll air-dry faster. My feet squish in my cleats as I make my way up to an open stool at the counter. I ring my cap out over the counter, mop the water up with a napkin, and place my hat gingerly back on my head. Frankie goes to sit by Arthur on the other end of our nine-person line. They're whispering furiously.

I order pistachio almond ice cream in a sugar cone. Jack, out of the "sheer goodness of his heart" purchases my treat for me. I nod appreciatively as I lick the delicious frozen dessert. I'm freezing cold (and shivering) but I don't say anything about it.

Out of nowhere all the lights shut off. The storm's knocked the power out. It's pitch black in the little eatery. I feel someone dry put their arm around me. It's kind of creepy, so I just move over to sit in the empty stool on the other side of me. I slip, though, because my shorts are wet, and fall on my tailbone on the hard tile floor.

"Dammit!" I gasp through the pain. As I try to grasp the counter and pull myself up, I hit my head on the ledge and then smash my elbow on the stool. I can't help myself, and I automatically cry out, "S##T." The guys all snicker. It's a good thing the only people in here are my teammates and the waiter.

After a while of whispering in the dark, the storm has ceased its incessant plundering. We agree it's safe to finally go home. And you better believe as soon as I get home I'm running right upstairs to take a long, hot bath. No questions asked. And in the silence and peacefulness of my luxurious bath, I just might be able to wrap my head around what happened this afternoon. Cuz right now, it feels like the only person who knows what the heck is going on in this world is none other than God Almighty. I think I need to have a talk with that guy.

CHAPTER 6

The Yard Sale

A week has passed, and with it brought new frustrations. For example, the punishments my mother gave me for the dress incident were A) fixing my dress (by which she means I had to cut the skirt portion of the dress off, sew a pink satin skirt and a layer of pale pink lace back onto it, until it looked almost identical to its pre-gravy state), B) not being allowed to listen to baseball games on the radio for one week (although I could still *play* baseball), and C) helping organize our yard sale to lighten our load for when we move to New York. The first part of my punishment gave me many puncture wounds on account of I have absolutely no sewing skills whatsoever; all I can say is thank God for sewing machines. The second part of my punishment was somewhat of a burden on Frankie, considering he would sit in his room, listen to the games, and flash the score (and other important baseball happenings) with his flashlight in Morse code over to me. The third punishment made me resent my mother, for she of all people knows I want nothing to do with this moving business. The fact of the matter is that no one will explain why we're moving. I just want one little answer, but I suppose that's too much to ask.

Anyways, so the yard sale today is starting at eleven o'clock and won't end until the last of our stuff has sold. The preparation I've gone through just for this one little yard sale can be summed up like this: I made advertisements and signs for it all over town, I set up a snack table that will hold iced tea, lemonade, vegetables and dip, cheese spread, crackers, and deviled eggs (all of which I contributed to greatly), I laid out all of the items we're selling, put price stickers on them, and last but not least, I must greet *every single person* that happens to stop by. The thing about Valia Springs is that yard sales are more than just yard sales - they're yet another social event in which all of the 500 valley inhabitants are obliged to attend. Needless to say, this was a Saturday that would not be spent playing baseball, although the rest of my team members are hanging out across the street in Frankie's backyard. That way, if their parents want them to go over to our yard sale they are close enough to; plus it's just plain old too hot to play baseball today, anyway.

By eleven thirty nearly the whole town is in our front yard, enjoying refreshments and chatting about the weather. It's cloudy today, and the smell of the breeze whispers *a storm is coming*. Looking at the sky, though, it is evident that this storm will not make its appearance until late evening. Meanwhile, ladies and gentlemen browse our for sale items dressed in their summer floral-print dresses and work suits with stiff collars. Their clothes, which presumably were freshly ironed this morning, have already started to wilt from the humidity, which is so thick it's almost difficult to breathe.

I'm to the point where the one hundred degree heat, combined with the humidity, makes my dress stick to my sweaty skin. To put it bluntly, it's as uncomfortable as rolling in a pool of molasses that smells like talcum powder. Between greeting people and making sales, I rush into the bathroom just to put baby powder on my underarms, shoulder blades, and feet. Then I rush back outside to shake my sticky hands with some other person. As you can imagine, I'm not having the best day. And this day happens to get worse when I hear the maniacal cackles of a certain Biff Richardson. Just what I need right now; a run-in with a guy as bright as a burned out light bulb. And he brought his gang members with him. Perfect.

My first instinct is to hide. This is how it is at school; I try to avoid Biff as much as possible. The first place I think to run to is the bathroom. Seeing as the path is blocked by shoppers, I duck under a fold-up table cluttered with our junk on top of it. Luckily there's a tablecloth on this table, so I'm relatively well-hidden. I see Biff's shoes from under the little gap between the tablecloth edge and the grass. He is snaking his way through the throngs of people at the snack table. His cohorts scatter and browse our stuff casually. Biff, seemingly unnoticed, makes his way over to the table I'm hiding under. I can see his shoes getting closer and closer…I sigh in relief when he walks right past my table.

"Hello, retard. Miss me this summer?" I hear Biff's voice before I see his face. I slowly turn around and look right into his face, inches from mine, peeking in from under the tablecloth. I scoot back when I realize he's coming under the table.

"Get out. Now." I wanted my voice to sound menacing and dangerous. Instead, it trembles and squeaks at the end. I gulp. Being under a table with Biff Richardson is the last place on Earth I want to be. I wonder how the adults could be so oblivious to what is going on; but I suppose there are so many people crowded together here, making quite a racket all trying to talk over each other, that practically *anything* could slip past them without a single person noticing.

"I heard you saw my brother Rocky a few weeks ago," he says in an eerily quiet voice. I don't want to ask, but I can't help myself.

"What are you talking about?" I question, gaining a little guts at the same time. My shaking is becoming more and more under control.

"You don't remember? He saw you at the junkyard with your little boyfriends. He wanted me to tell you that you should be a model, cuz you sure as Hell look good in a swimsuit." My heart stops cold for a moment. *Biff's brother was the Greaser staring at me? Why, I oughtta teach that kid to keep his brother's perverted thoughts to himself.* I'm ashamed to say it, but I didn't have the nerve to put up a fight. So the next best thing I could think of doing was run.

"What the Hell, you ugly b###h" he calls as I roll out from under the table, spring up, dash between the tables and fly across the street. I run into Frankie's backyard and shut the gate that separates most of the driveway from the backyard and garage. As my heart rate slows down, I take deep breaths to calm myself. I kind of panic every time I see Biff, on account of how intimidating he is; he shop-lifts, smokes, steals kids' lunch money, and he's been known to beat up a kid or two. All in all, if you knew him, you'd understand why avoiding him is always a good idea. But the thought that his brother, who's exactly like Biff but three years older, bigger, and scarier, was looking at me like that...it's just plain sick.

I slump onto the ground, my back leaning against the gate. I'm tired and don't wanna get up. There ain't nobody who's gonna make me work at that God-forsaken yard sale anymore, that's for sure.

The team has gathered around me, not saying anything, but just watching me. I hear footsteps on the pavement behind me, and I just know Biff is approaching. He always gets the last word.

"Hey! I wasn't finished with you yet!" he says loudly to me. Next comes the many clomps of his henchmen pounding up the driveway.

"Leave her alone, moron!" The command comes from JC. His hands are already balled into fists, prepared for a fight.

"I wouldn't be talkin', pipsqueak, or you'll be eatin' your own teeth," Biff retorts.

"Get outta here, Biff." This time, Frankie says it. His face was placid as he spoke.

"You can't tell me what to do."

"Yes I can. This is my property, and you're trespassing. Now I'm gonna count to three, and you better be gone by the time I'm finished. One...two... three." Biff doesn't so much as blink.

"Arthur, go call the cops for me." Frankie's dead serious. Just as Arthur gets into the house, Biff walks backwards down the driveway.

"Ya know what, fine. There's no need to get the police involved. See ya later, idiots. But you better be watchin' your back. I always give the last punch." And with that Biff and his buddies stalk off down the street, never to be seen by anyone ever again. And the team lived happily ever after. The end.

Yeah, right. I wish. This isn't a fairytale. And as my grandpa always says, 'things can only get worse before they get better.' How right he is.

CHAPTER 7

Unexpected Visitors

It's a few days later, not to mention the summer solstice. That's right, June 21st, the longest day of the year, and my goal is to spend every possible second of daylight playing baseball. I'm just walking out onto the front porch when Frankie comes strolling up the front steps.

"Hey, kid," he waves at me.

"Hey," I grin back, "what's up?"

"I've got great news," Frankie smiles, "Ricky's home! He came back real early this mornin'. I heard his car pull up, and when I went downstairs for breakfast today he was sleepin' on the couch."

"That's great! Penny's gonna be so happy when she hears." I hug him out of excitement, and in doing so feel that familiar shockwave. An awkward silence follows.

"Well, uh, we better start headin' to the field," Frankie says. So together we walk down to the diamond for another day of our favorite sport.

∾

Later in the morning, Frankie's up to bat, and like always, we move as far back as possible. JC, who always pitches to Frankie, is trying his hardest to get Frankie out. But so far, it's been three balls and no strikes. JC's confidence is waning faster than you can say "ball four", and it appears that Frankie is aware of this, so to make JC feel better in a not-so-obvious way, he swings at junk twice in a row. On the third time, however, he makes contact with the ball. And it sails past the infield, over the outfielders' heads, above the hill…and you can hear it hit the asphalt road behind the hill. It's an amazing homerun, but there's just one problem…that was the only baseball we brought today.

"God Dammit, Frankie, now we gotta go find the ball!" JC complains loudly.

"First of all, don't say 'God' in front of a swear word; it's a sin. Second, don't get your panties in a twist; it'll only take a minute to get the ball. You're just upset Frankie got a homerun off of you, as usual," Larry responds curtly. They start to get into an argument when I decide to intervene.

"Guys, knock it off, it's not a big deal. I'll go get it," I volunteer. This makes them (specifically JC) shut up. I take my mitt off, toss it on the ground, and jog toward the hill. I push myself up the relatively steep slope and take a quick breather at the top. Then, deciding I'll have a little fun while I'm over here, I roll down the hill horizontally. I used to do this a lot when I was younger, but I haven't in quite a while. It makes me extremely dizzy but it's still a ton of fun.

I stop rolling a few yards from the road. The baseball is peeking out of the tree line on the other side of the street. I go over and pick it up. The trees around me belong to the woods that the Pond is in, which explains why I smell cigarette smoke again. I turn away from the forest and shake the grass off of me from rolling down the hill.

"Where you goin' in such a hurry?" It's a guy's voice that comes from right behind me. Suddenly my arm's been taken hostage by a hot, clammy hand. I try to scream, but my mouth is covered by a second sweaty paw. I'm yanked backwards and my arms are tightly pinned against my back.

"Hey fellas, look who I just found on our turf," the person holding onto me calls. There's the snapping of branches and then a bunch of Greasers surround me, staring intently as if I were a steak or something.

"Nice find, Rocky. Whatta ya wanna do with her?" one of them says.

"Well, a pretty little girl like her shouldn't be out in the woods all alone…" Rocky replies in a sickeningly sweet tone.

"I say we take her with us, keep her safe, eh Red?" another guy laughs maliciously.

"I get her first," another declares.

"Shut up, meathead, I found her so I get her first," Rocky growls.

I stand there, completely frozen in terror, hyperventilating. My heart is thumping so loud it's vibrating my body. I feel like I'm gonna faint. I don't even wanna know what's gonna happen to me.

The boy named Red comes up to me. He crouches down 'til we're at eye level, strokes my face with the back of his hand and gazes into my eyes. I can't look away even though I desperately want to.

"Wish your boyfriend was here to join us," he whispers menacingly, a sly smile forming slowly on his face.

My body thaws so fast I can't believe my left leg has already left the ground. It swings fast and hard, as if it has a mind of its own, right into the place no man on

God's green earth ever wants to get hurt. Red's down, Rocky releases his grip in shock, and I bolt into the woods like a streak of lightning. I'm flying in between the trees and don't even consider stopping as I motor past the Pond. I can hear the group coming after me. Their shouts are getting closer. I sprint right up to the barbed wire-rimmed fence of the junkyard, not thinking, but just start climbing. I hurtle over the barbed wire and land hard on the dirt floor of the dump. My leg is bleeding pretty badly, but I don't stop running.

"There she is!"

"She's in the junkyard!"

"Get her!"

With the last of my adrenaline, I streak behind a large pile of garbage and dive under a beat-up car. The fence is being rattled aggressively at the entrance.

"Son of a b###h! The gate's got a new padlock on it!"

"Well, then just hop the fence!"

"Are you out of your mind, Joey? No one's stupid enough to do that!"

"Fine. We'll just sit here and wait 'til she comes out. She can't stay in there forever."

That's what I was afraid of.

∽

It's so dark I can't see my hand in front of my face. I've been laying still and silent for quite a few hours now. After the adrenaline went away, I practically went into a coma. Once I woke up, the sun was setting on the horizon. Before the sun went down completely, I heard the Greasers send a couple guys to "bring back some beverages" and they basically got drunk. I figure it's a safe time to come out from under the old car. I crawl out and slowly stand up, though I'm still a little bit shaky. I feel my way along a pile of garbage until I'm in view of the Greasers. The only reason I can tell where they are is because they're using their lighters to light up cigarettes.

The fact that they're drunk can be either a really good thing or a horrendously bad thing: a good thing because they're so intoxicated it'll be easy to escape and get home, but a bad thing because if I'm caught... well...I don't wanna think about it.

Managing to find my way to the back fence (although multiple times I've tripped on the junk) I take a deep breath and start climbing gingerly. I try to be quiet, but it's hard when your whole weight is on a chain-link fence. My hand, which is grasping for more of the fence, hits the barbed wire. So, very carefully, I swing one of my legs over it and shove my foot through one of the holes in the fence. It looks like I'm straddling the barbed wire, but my legs are pushing me up so I'm not actually touching the wire. Finally I get my other leg over with minimal pain and climb back down the other side.

Once my feet reach the ground I get on my hands and knees. I crawl on the dirt path, not really knowing where it's taking me, but trusting that it will lead me to somewhere familiar. Off in the distance, I can hear slurred shouts of the Greasers, mainly telling each other to pass them another bottle. Funny how they never say what's *in* the bottles.

The thin and slightly overgrown path I'm on takes a dead stop at the field surrounding the edges of my neighborhood. I stand up, realizing I'm hidden by the super tall grasses, and look around me. There are fireflies flitting around and a light shining not too far off. I head toward it, and I have a good feeling that it's someone's back porch light.

Something grabs the back of my shirt. That something turns out to be a hand. I scream so loud it hurts my own eardrums. I completely black out after that.

~

There's something cold on my forehead. I reach up to touch it, only to find that it's an icy, wet washcloth.

I'm not quite sure where I am, but wherever it is, it's kind of soft and comfy. My eyes peek open a tad. There's definitely light here, I can tell you that.

"I think she's waking up," someone says, and it couldn't be, but it sounds like...

"Grandpa?" I ask aloud. There's a great amount of shuffling noises and sighs of relief until I hear, closer to me now, "Yes, Charley. It's me. I'm here."

My eyes flutter open and Grandpa George is standing next to me. I try to sit up but he gently pushes me back down onto a pillow. I look around and it occurs to me that I'm on my front porch, lying on the wicker couch, surrounded by concerned looking family and friends. Two questions float through my still somewhat hazy mind: How did I get here? and, How long have I been out? Instead, I mutter groggily, "What happened?"

"That's what we would like to know," Grandpa replies.

"We was lookin' for ya all over town after you went to get the ball and never came back," Jack explains.

"We figured you were playin' a prank on us or somethin', but after a while we thought somethin' was wrong," JC adds.

"So we started a search party once it got dark. Then at around 11:15 I found you in the field yonder.

You screamed bloody murder when I tried to get your attention, then dropped like a rock, completely unconscious," Max continues.

"So the only question now is WHERE THE HECK WERE YOU THE PAST TWELVE HOURS?!?" Mother exclaims loudly, bemusing the boys, who are trying to restrain their chuckles.

"I don't want to talk about it right now. Maybe in the morning, if I feel better," I tell everyone quietly. Mother looks steamed, Father looks concerned, Grandpa looks troubled, Grandma Betsy looks sympathetic, and all the guys just stand there, averting their eyes.

"Can we go now?" JC whispers irritably to Frankie.

"Fine, go ahead," Frankie replies exasperatedly. Gradually the guys leave, one by one or two by two, until it's just Frankie and Arthur.

Grandma sits in the wicker chair next to me, holds my hand, and pleads quietly, "Please tell us what happened. Please." I really don't want to relive the day over again, but I'll do it for my grandparents.

I motion for Grandma to lend me an ear. She cocks her head close to my mouth and I murmur the story to her, keeping as many details out of it as possible. The whole time she listens the color drains from her face and her gentle sympathy turns into blatant horrification. Once I finish, she sits up slowly, clears her throat, and declares calmly, "It would be wise to report this to the authorities as soon as possible." Immediately everyone on the porch breaks out into a commotion of "What do you mean?"-s and "Why? What happened?"-s.

Grandma waits until everyone's silent, then says, "It would be best to discuss this in the house. Charlotte is emotionally exhausted at the moment, and probably needs a little time by herself on the couch here for a few moments anyway. I will explain the situation once inside."

Everyone follows her into the house after that, and I'm left to stare at the overhang above the porch. I close my eyes and try to relax. There seems to be absolute silence inside. Out of nowhere, there's a loud gasp, a rushing of footsteps, and an eruption of voices. Soon after, Arthur and Frankie come out onto the porch.

"We called the police station, but instead we got connected to Chief Richardson's house cuz no one was on duty at this hour. He said he'd take his deputy with him to investigate the crime scene," Arthur tells me. With any luck, the Greasers will still be there, drunk as ever. Getting the cops involved makes me remember that Chief Richardson is Rocky's uncle. How convenient.

"Well, see you tomorrow - uh - today, I mean," Arthur adds, making a reference to the time, and then makes his way down the porch steps and along the sidewalk to his house. Frankie's staring at me, a concerned look in his eyes.

"I got one word for you, kid: Wow. You escaped that by the skin of your teeth." I guess I know what he means; lately trouble seems to be following me like a black cloud. He comes and sits on the floor next to me.

"Are you okay?" he asks.

"I'm fine."

"No, seriously. They didn't hurt you, right?"

"Uh…not physically, no." I look down at my cut-up leg, which has neatly been cleaned of blood and wrapped snugly. "That cut was from climbing over the barbed wire fence," I remark.

"You're not allowed to go past those woods by yourself anymore. Your dad said so."

"Okay."

"We were all really worried, ya know."

"I know. By the way, how did I get back here?"

"You were…carried."

"By who?"

Frankie shrugs and replies, "No one in particular." He gets up and strides over to the stairs to the front walk, then abruptly turns to me.

"I just got a great idea," he smiles, "but it's a surprise. You better go on up to your room and get some rest now. See ya in a few hours." He strolls back across the street and up onto his front porch. Just before disappearing into the doorway, he turns and gives me one last wave. Then he vanishes into his house.

CHAPTER 8

Surprises

I finally awaken to find my drapes tightly drawn over the window in my bedroom and my little bedside clock telling me that it's one in the afternoon. Let it be known here that I've never been one to sleep in terribly late, so this sets my record for sleeping in. My bedroom is unusually dark and I note that I'm actually in my pajamas. Funny how I don't remember putting them on before climbing into bed. I get out of bed awkwardly and, after sleepily putting on fresh clothes, trod downstairs into the kitchen. I am absolutely STARVING considering I haven't eaten in over *twenty-four hours*. I slump into a chair at the table and am slightly stunned to find Grandpa sitting across from me, reading the newspaper, as if he did it every day of his life.

"Hello, Charley," he doesn't even look up from reading when he speaks, "you're just in time for lunch."

Just then Grandma sets two thickly stacked sandwiches on a plate in front of me. My mouth waters at the thought of food. I gobble up my lunch in an extremely uncivilized fashion. I'm just lucky Mother's not in the kitchen, or she'd scold me. As soon as I'm finished, Mother comes into the room.

"Some of your *friends* have been waiting for you on the porch," she tells me, then mumbles irritably to herself, "for the past three hours." I smile to myself. I've seriously got the best friends in the world. I kiss my grandparents on the cheek, say a quick goodbye, and head out the front door. On the way out I grab my mitt and bat.

"You seem to be recuperating quickly," Jack grins at me as I shut the screen door behind me.

"I guess," I shrug happily, "I suppose I just needed some sleep and food."

"Ya ready to go, Charley?" Arthur asks me.

"Yep! You guys didn't have to wait for me, you're too sweet..." I admit gratefully.

"Actually, we wanted to wait. We got somethin' special planned for this afternoon," Frankie says secretively.

"Okay, then. What is it?" I question.

"We're not telling you until we get there," Jack raises his eyebrows at me. I drop my mitt and bat and follow the three of them to the sidewalk.

"By the way, you might wanna ride your bike," Frankie advises me. I open the gate to the backyard, get it from its place leaning against the garage, walk it out to the sidewalk, close the gate, and hop on. The boys have already gotten onto their bikes, which were parked on my front lawn. I follow them down the street, around the corner, and keep pedaling all the way downtown. I honestly have no idea where we're going.

We've just passed the imaginary border line into the East Side of town when the guys skid to a stop. I pull up next to Arthur and look up at the Matinee Movie Theater sign proclaiming all-day showings of the premier of Walt Disney's brand-new movie, *Lady and the Tramp*. I completely forgot that the movie came out in theaters today; they've only had commercials for it on all the radio stations available in America.

I sigh and look exasperatedly at the three of them. Half-smiling, I say, "You've gotta be kidding me." My reaction is met by a bunch of "but it'll be nice"-s and I realize protesting their pleas would be completely in vain.

I sigh again and, in a last futile effort, ask half-heartedly, "Do I have to?"

"Yes!" they all exclaim, and with that, I am pushed through the doors of the theater.

"Four tickets to that new movie," Frankie tells the guy at the ticket window, handing him two dollar bills.

"Here ya go," the man mutters, handing Frankie the tickets. They have a large "2" on them, indicating we'll be viewing the movie in the second of the two screening rooms. I follow the three of them into the theater and slide into a seat between Jack and Frankie. Arthur's gone to get popcorn and soda. I settle into the itchy seat and wait for the show to start. The theater is packed. All throughout the dim room I can just barely identify people I know. There's some eleventh graders from my high school clustered in the very front row, and the little kids in my neighborhood are here with their parents. The room smells like butter, melted chocolate, and sweat. Arthur comes back and slides down the row into the seat next to Frankie. We're sitting all the way in the top back row, the only people in this section. Suddenly the lights go out, and the music starts playing, and the huge movie screen begins to glow. I'm almost instantly enthralled by the whole production. Leaning back, I notice that Frankie's got his arm stretched across the back of my seat. I shift closer to him and feel that shockwave the millisecond our knees touch. My mind is going crazy, screeching *Oh my gosh, oh my gosh, oh my gosh!* so loud you'd wonder if he could hear it, our heads are so close together. I try to relax, take a deep breath, and focus on the movie.

〜

Once the movie ends, my jaw has dropped and my eyes are wide.

"That…was…so…*CUTE!*" I squeal loudly, causing Frankie to pull his arm back in surprise. The other people in the theater are clapping vigorously, but some turn and glare at me awkwardly because of my outburst. I blush and sink low into my chair. Whoops. I forgot it was a crime to be happy in this town.

The extra large popcorn tub we all shared is completely empty, except for the kernels, of course. If we had taken Danny, Max, Larry, or JC with us, those kernels would have been used as ammo to be shot out of drinking straws. And then we probably would have gotten kicked out of the theater. So I can see why we didn't bring them. But it seems all boys have absolutely ravenous appetites, so it's no wonder why I barely got any popcorn while Arthur and Jack basically ate the whole thing. Frankie tried to be polite and save a bunch for me, but there was no stopping the other two once the popcorn was passed to them.

"I'm glad you liked it," Jack smiles at me as all the other people start to get up and exit.

"I gotta admit, it was much better than I thought it would be," Frankie says.

"Are you kidding? That was the cheesiest crappy animated dog romance movie I've ever seen!" exclaims Arthur.

"But it's the *only* animated dog romance movie you've ever seen, so you have nothing to compare its subjective cheesiness or crappiness to," I explain to him.

"Yeah, well, it's still lame. And no one can convince me otherwise." Frankie shoots him a look. "Well, no one except that kid," he says slightly louder so Frankie can hear what he just announced.

"You are such a kiss-up," I roll my eyes at him.

I didn't realize it, but everyone else is gone. The guy who sweeps the theater floor yells at us to leave. We all sheepishly make our way out of the cinema. We get on our bikes and start pedaling back to our neighborhood when I remember something.

"Hey Frankie, I just was thinkin' about how I haven't gotten to see Ricky yet," I say.

"He should be at home still. He's mainly been resting the last two days, but once Penny heard he was back she's been takin' work off to see him. She'll probably be at my house, too," he replies.

Jack goes back to his house once we reach our street. Arthur drops his bike off at his house and then jogs after me and Frankie until we reach our houses. To our surprise, Ricky is in my driveway, bent under the open hood of my granddad's rust-colored Chevy pick-up truck, some oil stains on his white tank top and jeans, a greasy rag tucked into his back pocket. Penny is sitting in a chair on the corner of my porch closest to him, and it appears that they are chatting with each other. This is a very strange scene, especially since neither one of them has noticed that the three of us showed up (or, if they did notice, they're not letting on).

Frankie clears his throat loudly, and the sound makes Ricky and Penny turn to us.

"We ain't interruptin' somethin', are we?" Frankie asks them earnestly.

"No, not at all," answers Ricky, but Penny jumps in and explains, "We were just discussing wedding plans, that's all." She says it in a dreamily happy, soft voice. Ricky stops whatever it is that he's doing and comes over to us.

"Hi there, Arthur! Are you excited for twelfth grade in the fall?" Ricky asks him, referring to the fact that Arthur is two grades ahead of me and Frankie.

"I guess," Arthur shrugs amiably. Ricky nods and smiles and turns to me.

"Well, look who it is," he says to me, "how ya doin', kid?" He's like a close cousin to me, really.

"Fine, I suppose," I admit lightly.

"Well it's good to know you're still keepin' an eye on my brother for me. He'd probably get in a lotta trouble if it weren't for you," he jokes, "but then again, I hear you've got enough trouble on your own plate. Penny's been tellin' me 'bout how you're movin' and what happened yesterday and the dress incident."

"Oh, yeah, well..." I mumble sheepishly. Jeez, it's like the whole town knows there's something wrong with me. Ricky reaches out and ruffles my hair...and then it hits me.

"MY HAT'S GONE!" I cry in shock. I can't believe I hadn't noticed earlier, but now that I think about it, I haven't worn it the whole day.

"Oh my gosh, you're right!" Arthur exclaims in a totally non-serious, laughing kind of way, "I *knew* somethin' seemed different 'bout you today."

"You had it on last night when I left," Frankie states. I try to think back to when I went to bed. I always put my hat on my bedpost when I take it off, but I don't recall it being there when I woke up...

"I'm gonna go check my room," I declare, then dash up the front steps and through the doorway. I get stopped dead in my tracks when I discover the foyer filled with flower bouquets, a stack of envelopes higher than the Appalachians, and every pie and cake imaginable.

"Thank Heaven you're finally home," Mother sighs, briskly striding through the living room entryway. "I was wondering when I'd be able to get your sympathy presents out of the way."

"Sympathy presents?" I inquire.

"Yes, honey. All afternoon ladies from town have been stopping by to drop off gifts for you. I suppose they all feel the need to help you 'get better' after yesterday's incident," she responds. "Well, go on. Take them upstairs," she commands curtly.

"I'll help you with that," Grandpa states as he appears seemingly out of nowhere. Mother frowns.

"Really, George, it isn't necessary, especially in your state…" she protests.

"Nonsense, Judy. It's no trouble at all," he replies, and with that, we've each grabbed as many flower-filled vases as we can carry. We take them up to my room and set them down on the floor over by the window. I glance at my bedposts, but to my dismay, my Yankees cap isn't there. Shoot. Grandpa and I continue taking things up to my room.

"Hey Grandpa, why's Ricky workin' on your truck? Did it break down or somethin'?"

"Actually, the engine was feeling a little shaky and the transmission was taking a little too long to start up," he explains casually. He sets down two more vases, both filled with carnations.

"Wait, then why did you come visit us? I mean, we always drive to your home, but why are you here? And what time did you get here yesterday?"

"Well, we got here around three o'clock yesterday, to answer your third question. As for your second question, your Grandmother and I felt we should help you get ready for moving. Not to mention we wanted to be here to celebrate your birthday with you."

"But I don't even want to move! So your help is just adding fuel to a flame I want to put out as soon as possible. And no one will tell me *why* we're moving in the first place!" I exclaim exasperatedly.

"I'm sure your parents will explain why you're moving soon enough." The way he says this last sentence with such finality communicates to me that this discussion is over.

We've just taken the last armful of stuff up to my room and are coming back down the stairs. Grandpa looks winded and tired from all the lifting and climbing. He shouldn't overexert himself at his age, so I make him go sit in the living room. He gingerly sets himself down on our old La-Z-Boy recliner and stares out the window. Grandpa seems sort of gloomy, but I just can't put my finger on it. The hot afternoon sunlight streams through the open picture window in front of us and heats a large spot of carpet where Ginger is sleeping. The sunlight makes her copper-colored fur glow to a bright orangey-gold. All she really ever does is sleep, considering my parents got her as a marriage gift and she's like sixteen years old (that's 112 in dog years, for your information). She is very much my mother's dog, and as you can imagine when she first got Ginger she spent nearly every waking moment trying to train the puppy into a serene, respectable dog. I guess it worked, because Ginger is one of the most obedient dogs I know. She's pretty peaceful; she doesn't steal food, doesn't dig up the backyard, and is very amiable. Her only quirks are that she loves to bark at anyone and anything at anytime, all the time (she's kind-of stopped the *incessant* barking but still barks quite a bit)and she likes to curl up on furniture with my parents (like the couch or their bed).

Just then, Father arrives home from work. Today is Friday, which explains why he's home from work early; it's the only workday he gets out an hour earlier than usual. He has to park on the street because our driveway is blocked by Grandpa's truck. Penny, Ricky, Arthur and Frankie are still hanging out in my front yard and wave to my father as he makes his way into the house.

"Good afternoon, Father," he says cordially to Grandpa, then sits down in a chair to read our local newspaper's Friday evening news. When he unfolds it I'm taken aback to see the front-page headline, which reads,

"*Adolescent Gang Arrested for Holding Teenage Girl Hostage*". There's a large photo under it which shows the drunken lot of the Greasers sprawled around the gate to the junkyard entrance. Beer bottles and cigarette butts are scattered randomly all around them. Now isn't this just dandy?

"Mother, Judy, you might want to come see this," calls Father. The two women appear in the doorway in aprons, which explains the smell of dinner wafting through the house.

"What is it, dear?" asks my mother.

"Look at the front page of the newspaper," he replies solemnly. Her eyes widen and her face goes slack. Grandma just utters a quiet, "Oh, my," and Grandpa frowns.

"I can't believe those scums at the printing press have the *gall* to write about such a terrible, traumatizing event, concerning our daughter, without our consent!" cries Mother.

"Please read it aloud for me, Son," Grandpa requests.

Father clears his throat and begins, "*At approximately 12:08 am on June 22nd, Police Chief Gerry Richardson received a phone call from Mr. David Mason, requesting the Chief's presence at the entrance to the junkyard tucked back in the woods behind the Wilson Street neighborhood. Chief Richardson took* *with him Deputy Stanley Kowalski. They arrived on the scene at approximately 12:23 am, and upon arrival, discovered eight young men, all aged either 16, 17, or 18 years old, intoxicated by the junkyard's entrance. A total of 32 bottles of beer and 51 cigarettes were found around the premises. Chief Richardson had them all put under arrest for underage drinking and put them in the Police Station's holding cell overnight. According to Chief Richardson, Mr. David Mason had called to report that his nearly fifteen-year-old daughter, Miss Charlotte Mason, had been cornered on the edge of the woods around 11:30 am by the same group of adolescent boys found at the crime scene. According to Mr. Mason, the young men had "said some extremely threatening things to her, and it was greatly implied in everything they said that they were going to defile her". They then, according to Mr. Mason, had chased her through the woods until she was able to climb over the junkyard fence and hide under an old car. They supposedly were waiting her out by the padlocked junkyard entrance. She finally made her escape at approximately 11:00 pm by climbing back over the fence and making her way home in the dark. When questioned about this story, the young men (which chose not to have their names printed) claimed they had no idea that Miss Mason was hiding inside the junkyard. Evidence has yet to be found that supports the story Mr. Mason gave over the phone. However, the boys will be in the holding cell until Monday morning or until they come up with the bail money ($500) as a punishment for their lawless alcohol consumption. When asked if he believed Mr. Mason's account, Chief Richardson replied, "I am inclined to believe his story because [generally] people wouldn't call about those kinds of situations without it being 100 percent* *serious. Deputy Kowalski and I are going to investigate under and around this car that Miss Mason reportedly hid under, just to make sure she was actually there. Then we'll have evidence to back Mr. Mason's story."*

Once Father has finished reading, Mother is the first to respond.

"They act as if we made up the whole story for publicity or something," she says incredulously.

"Whoever wrote this article is probably just trying to save the reputation of the boys who did this to Charlotte," Grandma adds.

"It says here that the article was written by Paul Solomon, and if I'm not mistaken, his son was one of the boys involved in this whole fiasco," Father mentions.

"I've kept this to myself long enough, but now I'm positive those East-siders have it out for us West-siders," Mother admits. "I knew it was a mistake when we bought this house instead of the other one we looked at on the East side, even if it was a lot more expensive."

"Well, it doesn't matter anymore because we'll be moving soon enough and we'll never have to come back here again," declares Father. I can't take it anymore, the suspense is *killing* me!

"FOR THE LOVE OF GOD, WHY ARE WE MOVING?!" I shout. My sudden outburst has left everyone else in the room speechless, and the people on my front lawn have stopped what they're doing; apparently I forgot that the living room window opens up to the front porch.

"Wh-wh-what do you mean?" Father stammers.

"You know very well what I mean. I have asked again and again and *again*, but no one will give me a straight answer. I'm a part of this family, too, and I deserve to know why out of nowhere I come home and find out we're moving away for some mysterious, untold reason. You can't keep it a secret forever!" My voice has died down from shouting, but is still kind of loud. I'm just in general a very loud person, I guess.

"Go ahead. Tell her," Grandpa commands quietly, his eyebrows furrowing in concentration. My parents exchange glances. Finally Grandma, who's now quite teary-eyed, opens her mouth. Her voice trembles when she speaks.

"We found out several weeks ago that your grandfather has leukemia, and as we all know I'm getting too old to take care of him by myself. So I tried to convince each of your Father's seven siblings to come move in with us to help me care for Grandpa, and your father, bless his heart, was the only one of his brothers and sisters who made the huge sacrifice to uproot you and your mother to come take care of us…" her voice trails off. She can't talk anymore because she's broken out into silent sobs. Mother puts her arm around Grandma's shoulders to comfort her, then leads her to the couch and helps her sit down. Father and Grandpa just look down. I feel like an idiot and a jerk. My eyes well up with tears and my throat burns. My bottom lip starts to quiver. And that's when I run. I run out of the living room, I run down the hallway, I run through the kitchen, I run out the back door, I run out the back gate of my backyard, I run through the field filled with tall grasses, I run and run and run until I just can't run anymore, and my knees buckle and I fall to the ground, crying my eyes out. I don't think I can take anymore. I'm breathing shakily and my body won't stop convulsing, not to mention my shirt is soaked from my own tears. I look up suddenly and realize right where I am. I'm at the stream that runs from the mouth of Valia Springs, the water source that my town is named after. The stream runs along the outline of the mountains surrounding the valley and leaves the mountains a long ways away, where it becomes a waterfall. The other end of the stream, where I am, goes back through a nearby holler to the springs. I decide to follow the stream up into this holler (otherwise known as the Jacksons' Holler) until I'm at the very springs themselves. There are a bunch of boulders everywhere, but one particularly large one captures my attention. Someone painted a huge cross on the surface of the rock and wrote under it, "Jesus Guides the Way." I think whoever did this was referring to the way the spring and creek flows through our valley, but it just seems appropriate to kneel before the painting. I start murmuring lots and lots of prayers, every prayer I've ever learned from school, in fact (I never thought I'd say this, but thank God for Sister Sean making us memorize every prayer in our fifth grade prayer book). I just keep praying and praying, and then I go back and do over all the prayers I've already said a second and third time. Call me crazy, but I guess when you've hit rock bottom the only place to go is up.

"Are you OK?" Frankie asks me as he appears from behind a boulder. I have a questioning look on my face, but instead of asking how he found me I simply reply, "I'm a lot better than I was an hour ago."

He looks me over, then his eyes roam over the giant painting of the cross. "Oh crap, I'm sorry. I didn't mean to disturb your praying," he says apologetically.

"It's no big deal. I was pretty much finished anyway. So how did you find me?"

"I heard the conversation going on in your living room through the open window. Then I heard you run out the back door and gate. It was obvious you were in the field; the tricky part was trying to locate you within the field. Once I came upon the creek I followed it. And here we are now."

"So you know about the newspaper article...and the other thing..." I try not to elaborate on the things

I desperately want to forget. He runs his hand through his hair nervously.

"You've been crying." It's a statement, not a question. I quickly wipe any leftover tears away with the back of my hand. "I'm really sorry, Charley. About the incident yesterday, and about your Grandpa. I know how hard it can be when someone you love is really sick... anyways, I'll take you home whenever you're ready."

"I guess we can go now. I don't really need to stay here any longer." He lends me his hand and pulls me up off of my knees. Neither of us lets go, though, as we make our way back through the field. The sadness I was feeling is replaced by the lovely euphoria of his hand in mine. My whole arm is tingling with joy. It's not until we're almost out of the field that he finally releases my hand, and when he does, I'll admit that I'm disappointed it ended.

We get back onto the concrete that makes up our street. Penny, Ricky, and Arthur are gone. Everything is still and quiet.

"I'll see you tomorrow, I guess," I say to him quietly, then I go over and climb up the trellis to my window. I lost my appetite quite a while ago, and I really don't feel like encountering my family anymore tonight. They'll eventually check to see if I'm in my bedroom, but by then I'll be fast asleep. I get in my pajamas and lay in bed. It really can't get any worse. I'm just hoping things get better from here.

CHAPTER 9

Max's Day

My hat is still missing, which is very disheartening because I feel naked if I'm not wearing it. I've looked absolutely everywhere; I've scoured my house and bedroom, my porch, garage, backyard, Father's car, Grandpa's truck, the movie theater, the junkyard (well, the guys did that one for me, considering I'm not allowed at the Pond or anywhere near the dump anymore), the baseball diamond we play at, the ice cream shop, even Dee-Dee's Diner. It's fallen off the face of the Earth, and I just need to stop obsessing over it and move on, JC explained to me bluntly. For once I took his advice.

On a better note, today is Max's day to spend with me. He decided the ideal place to go is his favorite place in the world, Dee-Dee's. Yes, my special day spent with Max will consist of an all-expenses-paid-by-him lunch at the local diner. How original.

He picks me up at 11:30 and we ride our bikes there. We sit down at the counter like we always do, and as usual, Penny is our waitress. To start off, we order a large basket of French fries, along with a chocolate malt for Max and a strawberry malt for me. Penny keeps talking to us about the details of her upcoming wedding. My family got invited, but we doubt we'll be attending because, of course, the wedding's in early August and by that time we'll already have moved. Penny is describing her wedding dress, which is getting shipped in from Atlanta, when our fries and malts come out of the kitchen. We interrupt her bubbly babbling to order our entrees. I get a simple corned beef and sauerkraut sandwich on rye bread, adding a pickle and potato chips on the side. Max, on the other hand, gets a bacon, lettuce and tomato sandwich *and* a double-decker cheeseburger with potato chips as a side dish. Max is pretty chubby, but whenever the other guys tease him about it, he tells them he's just in a growth spurt. "*Yeah, a growth spurt that lasts 15 years,*" JC once retorted to Max's constant excuse. I whacked him on the shoulder for that comment. It's not Max's fault that he's only five-foot-four and hasn't grown since seventh grade. He's actually kinda sweet, once you get past his permanently-growling stomach.

Penny brings us our food and continues on with her excited chattering. She wanted me to be one of the junior bridesmaids, but I explained to her my dilemma and she told me that she understood, that she would just find someone else, and she was sorry I couldn't be there. After a brief silence, she resumes the details of how many people will be there ("As many as St. John the Apostle's Church can hold!" she exclaims), who will cater the reception afterwards ("Ricky's Uncle Salvatore is doing the whole dinner for free!"), the honeymoon details ("We're spending two weeks in Miami!") and, finally, the house those two will move into ("It's the most adorable little cottage a quarter mile out of town, plenty of outdoor space, and an extra bedroom that can easily be turned into a nursery when necessary...").

Max is completely devouring his food but seems to be listening to Penny attentively. I finished my lunch a while ago, but he's just now finished off the sandwich, the cheeseburger's already gone, there are no chips left and he ate the rest of the French fries before his main dishes even arrived. You can imagine I'm mildly surprised when he orders two rice puddings for our dessert. I absolutely *love* rice pudding, and by the way Max is gobbling it up you can tell he likes it too.

I've just swallowed the last heavenly bite of my dessert when Max nudges me with his elbow. He's nodding over his shoulder. I turn to glance in that direction, and what I find is greatly distressing. Biff and his gang have just entered the diner and are crowded in the extra large corner booth next to the jukebox. I nearly choke on my bite of pudding at the sight of them, and Max has to pat me roughly on the back to get me to stop coughing. Unfortunately, this has brought unwanted attention to us, and as you can guess Biff has spotted us. Instinctive avoidance starts to make its way through my body.

"Let's go to the diamond," I command under my breath. Max nods in agreement and throws the money we owe on the counter. We dash out of the restaurant and to our bikes. I've just hopped on mine when I hear Biff call from behind me, "Hey! Stupid! You and me need to have a little talk!" I start pedaling with Max right beside me.

"Hey! Are you *deaf?* I'm talkin' to you!" Biff shouts.

"Pedal faster," Max murmurs. We take off at top speed to the baseball field. Too bad Biff and his cronies are hot on our trail. I am *so* sick of Biff ruining *everything* that could have been a good occasion! Why doesn't he just leave me *alone?*!

That's when I get the sensation of déjà vu. It seems like I'm always running away from *something*, and then the problems I retreat never get resolved. It's becoming a repetitive pattern. Well you know what? That pattern ends today. I'm done running. Enough is enough.

We get to the diamond quickly. I drop my bike and sprint to the safe haven that is the dugout. Max, who happens to be very slow, finally makes it over to the group of boys gathered around the dugout, panting.

"What the Hell is going on *now?*" JC complains exasperatedly.

"Biff showed up at the diner and followed us here," I grumble. The guys break out in angry exclamations about how that moron can't leave well enough alone.

"Why if it isn't the Wicked Witch of the West-Side," calls Biff, who's strutting over to home plate with bodyguards on either side of him. The sound of his voice makes the hair on the back of my neck stand up, as if my body knows there's going to be a fight here one way or another. He seems to have appeared out of nowhere. "We have some unfinished business to attend to," he says pointedly at me, "you got my brother arrested. So you better pay the price or suffer the consequences." Simultaneously his henchmen crack their knuckles in what is supposed to be an intimidating way. It's like something straight out of the mafia.

"Back off. You're outnumbered, not to mention we have weapons," Frankie glares at him. By weapons, he was referring to our baseball bats. JC, who's grasping his, holds it horizontally and repeatedly lets it smack the palm of his hand.

"Just give me the little bi –"

"I swear on my mother's grave if you lay a finger on her I'll–"

"Stop!" I exclaim, grabbing both boys' attention. I lock eyes with Frankie and state firmly, "This is *my* battle." He holds my gaze for a long time but reluctantly nods in agreement.

A bully, troublemaker, and rich kid all rolled into one; this fact puts nearly every kid in fear of Biff. Except for just plain stupid people, nobody would mess with him. Until now. And with all the courage within me, I stroll right up to Biff. Alone.

I'm about to ask what the Hell he could possibly want from me when he spits in my face. Not an ordinary spit, but a loathing wad of eerily warm, spite-filled saliva. I wipe it away with my T-shirt sleeve. Biff steps toward me and raises his hand as if to slap me. It sails through the air, but at the last second I block it with my fist. But my fist didn't stop there. It flew through the air and landed square in his face. I heard a thud but barely felt the reverberating pain when knuckles meet skull. Biff stumbles back, and with every ounce of strength in my body, every single fiber of my entire being, I rammed into him, knocking him onto his back on the ground... and I went down with him, kicking and punching and screaming words that should never be repeated all at the same time. Something in me had snapped, and there was no way in Heaven or Hell I was ever gonna take crap from him again. He was wailing for me to stop, shrieking for mercy, but for once *I* wasn't finished with *him* yet. His goons tried to pull me off, but I thrashed so much that they couldn't get a grip on me. Every mean thing he'd ever said or did to me passed through my mind, becoming fuel to a raging wildfire that I couldn't control. Hot, sticky blood oozed from his broken nose and splattered on my clothing, fists, and arms.

Finally Frankie grabs a hold of the back of my shirt collar. He tugs at it a little and I get up off of Biff. I step back and survey the damage I caused.

Biff is whimpering as he struggles to get up. The blood streaming from his nose runs down his mouth to his saturated shirt. Both his eyes are black, a tooth is missing (although I think it was missing before this), and his appendages are covered in yellow, green, blue, pink, and purple bruises.

"You- You- You better bet I'll tell the police you did this," he stutters.

"Okay, go ahead. Tell the police that a girl beat you up. Your reputation will be ruined, and every kid will know that you're not nearly as tough as you think are," I say calmly. Biff seems to think this through.

"F-f-fine, but if I don't talk, you don't talk," he replies. Then he limps away with his thugs. I'm finally free of Biff Richardson's incessant torture.

Now if only I could say the same thing about the Pretty Posse…

CHAPTER 10

The Fourth of July

Today's the fourth of July, so the whole town's having its annual potluck barbecue at the park by the baseball field. There's a small playground (with a slide, swings, and a merry-go-round that you push to make it go fast and then jump on) for the younger kids to play on, and plenty of picnic tables to eat at. You probably guessed this already, but it's yet *another* gimmick used to get the townsfolk to interact with each other. The possibilities and opportunities for social events here are endless.

Grandma and Mother have been slaving over a hot oven all day baking Grandma's famous, award-winning Georgia peach pies. They've made six so far today. They normally wouldn't be putting so much pressure on themselves to make the pies absolutely flawless, but when potlucks are in the town's upcoming future it's an unspoken competition to see which lady can bring the best food item. But now that Grandma's in town, she's brought on a whole new level to the competition; because she used to visit us in Valia Springs so frequently she holds a legacy for being a fantastic cook. All the women in town are gonna be working their butts off to try to make better food than her, always to no avail. Why they feel the need to turn a simple potluck into a mindless ballyhoo is beyond my comprehension.

My father, on the other hand, started out a leisurely morning by reading the Atlanta Journal-Constitution. I skimmed through it after he was done reading it, but it's always the same thing over and over: it's always either about President Eisenhower and the nuclear bomb threat from the Soviet Union, or about the huge bus boycott going on in Montgomery, Alabama. After immersing himself into the latest national happenings, he mowed the lawn with his old push mower; that gave him an hour to deeply engross himself in thought, as usual. Now he's upstairs getting ready for this afternoon, probably deciding which button-up shirt to choose: the white one with the thin, faded red pinstripes or the striking midnight blue one with the collar that constantly curls under. Both are patriotic, and both look somewhat ridiculous. Decisions, decisions.

I, lastly, was forced to wear my pink dress because apparently a holiday potluck/barbecue is something to dress up all fancy for. I even have to wear these dainty white gloves, lest my fingertips brush the infectious disease-ridden public picnic tables. So guess who gets to play baseball in her Church dress?

Grandpa and I have been sitting on the front porch talking all day. Grandpa was sweet enough to get me a little Independence Day gift, a new pack of baseball cards. I only got three cards I didn't already have, but it's the thought that counts.

"Are you going to play baseball when we get to the picnic?" he asks.

"Yep," I reply.

"I know you've told me a thousand times before, but what position do you play?"

"Third base."

"That's real neat," he smiles, "because I used to play third base for the Yankees back in the day."

"I *know* that already, Grandpa," I sigh exaggeratedly, "why do you think that's my favorite position?" His eyes gleam with pride when I admit this.

"Anyways, I think I'll watch you kids play for a little while. I've wanted to observe your skills for quite some time." After that Grandpa turns on the radio and tunes into the Yankees game. We listen until Mother informs that it is, in fact, time to leave. By then it's the top of the third inning, and the Red Sox are up by two.

We get to the park and already there's tons of food: potato salad, pasta salad, fruit salad, egg salad, regular salad, coleslaw, corn on the cob, watermelon, hotdogs, ice cream, hamburgers, submarine sandwiches as long as the picnic table they're on, and pies every color of the rainbow. Of course, Grandma's pies are *always* the best.

The sky is the most picturesque shade of blue and has the perfect balance of white, fluffy clouds that pop out in a very three-dimensional way. It's easy to make shapes out of them. I've seen two that reminded me of puppies, one that looked like a turtle and one that appeared to be a windmill. It's beautifully warm and there's a breeze. For once the humidity isn't stifling the breath out of me.

Slipping off my white gloves (because obviously I won't be using them for baseball), I meet up with the guys, most of which are already playing baseball. Luckily, this is the mingling hour, which means that we have one hour of distraction-free playing while everyone else chats before dinner commences. The boys are wearing nice enough clothes that would be considered appropriate for the picnic, and yet they can still manage to play baseball without looking too absurd. I, of course, stick out like a sore thumb. Despite many uncomfortable stares and quite a bit of teasing and chuckles from the guys, I manage to get over my self-consciousness and play with my usual enthusiasm (though I do make an effort to not slide to any of the bases or risk tearing/dirtying my dress, not to mention I'd receive the wrath of Mother).

Through the course of this hour, I happen to get two singles, an intentional walk, and a double, not to mention I catch three pop flies and tag Larry out for trying to steal third. Grandpa sits at a picnic table facing the field and watches us play, smiling the whole time.

"You're pretty good, Charley," Grandpa says to me, "and so's that Italian boy. You two are the best on the team." I know he's trying to be nice and all, but I'm really not that good. I'm OK at bats, and I can catch almost anything, but my throwing is *way* off. It's either above the guy's head or at his feet.

I grab some fruit salad and a hotdog and join Frankie at an unoccupied picnic table. He's eating a slice of sub sandwich, potato salad, and two heaping watermelon slices. Not to mention my grandma gave him a whole pie all to himself. "Such a nice boy," she always says about him, but we all know she just feels pity towards him because his mom died when he was seven.

"Nice pie," I joke, "hungry at all?"

"Starving! I didn't eat all day just to save room for this," he smiles.

The rest of the boys come over and sit down, and we talk and laugh and eat. Dinner ends and unfortunately we can't finish our game because the fireworks will be starting in a few minutes. Dusk has fallen, the fireflies are starting to come out, and I decide to climb up this oak tree to get a better view of the fireworks. I've only made my way up three branches (yes, in a dress, but before you panic I'll tell you I'm wearing bloomers on underneath it. *Yes,* unfortunately I am forced to wear *bloomers*) when I discover Frankie's already up there, sitting in my spot.

"Hey, what're ya doin' up here?" I ask.

"Tryin' to get a better view. You?"

"Same." Luckily there's room for the both of us if we sit right next to eachother. No complaints here.

"Hey, tell your Grandma thanks for the pie. It was real delicious, and I should know, seeing as all my relatives make four star meals everyday."

"Oh, sure. It wasn't a big deal. She likes you, ya know."

"Yeah, but it's only cuz my mom's gone." His deep brown eyes are looking off into the distance. This is the face he always gets when he thinks about his mother. There's a long silence.

"Frankie, look, I'm sorry –"

"Don't worry about it. I just wanna enjoy watching the fireworks and sitting alone up here with you."

The sun sinks below the horizon, leaving the sky tiered with gold, orange, yellow, pale rose, lilac, and cerulean. Fireworks are erupting high above the sunset, splashing the darkening sky with patriotic colors and raining down streams of sparks. The light radiating from them is so fantastic that it illuminates everything around it, giving my view of Frankie a soft glow every time there is an explosion. It is so perfect that I lean in and so does Frankie, and I close my eyes and turn my head just so; 'This is it!' my mind screamed. I could just barely feel his lips...

CRACK!!! A firework so loud it could've caused an earthquake made us jump back. I blushed and he turned his head away and ran his fingers through his hair. The perfect first kiss that could've been was ruined. We watched the rest of the fireworks in awkward silence.

CHAPTER 11

Larry's Day

Two days later the carnival arrives. It comes every year but is only here for the first full weekend of July. Three days of junkfood, cheap rides, and carnie rip-offs. Not my ideal place to go, mainly because I'll most likely run into some jerk or brat from my school, but of course it's exactly where Larry decides to take me. Not that I don't like carnivals; it's just that they've lost their luster over the years. I've been to the fairs so many times that they don't seem nearly as fun or magical anymore.

"This is what I look forward to every summer," Larry tells me as we approach the ticket booth. It's noon on the rarely busy Main Street, where a clock tower chimes 12:00pm and people bustle around excitedly. We order cotton candy, funnel cakes, and cracker jacks as our lunch from sweaty, greasy vendors. Luckily the food is good, though I try not to think about the people serving it. If I did I probably wouldn't be eating my lunch.

"So whadda ya wanna do?" Larry asks me once we finish. I know for sure there's one thing I want to do

–go on the Ferris wheel. But I'm stalling until it's dark to go on it because by then it'll be beautifully lit up.

"Um, how 'bout the balloon darts?" I suggest.

"Sure! And after that I - I mean we - can do the duck shooting game! And of course we'll do the ball-in-the-fishbowl game too. You could get a cool goldfish or somethin', and then we'll go to the fun house and the giant slide and the pendulum ride…" he just goes on and on. For once someone is more talkative than I am. Larry talks enough for the two of us, and *that* is saying something. Larry's not much taller than me, really skinny (which helps him be fast), and has light brown hair with blue eyes. He's not unattractive, although if you ask me he only thinks about himself. Hopefully he'll grow out of this.

The warm, breezy afternoon wafts with the smells of carnival foods, oily rides, and the sweaty, sticky smell you get when too many people are crowded together in too small of an area. The afternoon is filled with every traditional carnival activity, from knocking over the bottles with a baseball, to using a giant hammer to try to hit the bell. Afternoon faded into evening by the time we did every single activity – except the Ferris wheel. I guess everyone else had the same idea I did (to wait until it was dusk) so I and Larry (oh, and my new fish Scarlett, who's swimming in her tiny fishbowl) start to make our way through the crowd to get in line. As we stroll down Main

Street the whole fair lights up with every color of the rainbow in neon. Every single thing glows and shines like you wouldn't believe, and music starts playing over the speakers that are set up everywhere. It is a catchy song that sounds familiar, but considering I hardly ever am allowed to listen to modern music, I don't know what it is called. I ask Larry, who swiftly informs me that it is "Life Could Be a Dream" by The Crew Cuts. Yeah, I've never heard of it. But it is still perfect for the moment. It was the kind of song that makes your head bob side to side and before you know it you're snapping your fingers to the beat.

We trod down the pavement, basking in all the magic of the pitch black mixed with bright lights. We finally get in the unusually long line for the Ferris wheel. While we wait for our turn, another catchy song comes on the speakers. This one, luckily, I have heard; it's "Mr. Sandman" by the Chordettes. I mouth the chorus with the song. Larry gives me an odd look, like it's weird to lip-synch in public. If you ask me, I think he cares too much about what other people think.

After what seems like an eternity we get our own box. We get strapped in behind a metal bar, and off we soar much faster than I was anticipating. It is magical – blackness except for a sky filled with stars and the amazing array of lights from the carnival below us. It is like something out of a movie. The only thing missing is…. Frankie.

I feel awful after I think that. Larry is still pretty cool. Why wasn't he good enough?

We are at the very top of the ride when Larry makes a good observation.

"We've stopped." He says it like a confusing yet surprising question. I notice it too. Suddenly people from below us start talking loudly and shouting.

"What happened?"

"Is something wrong?"

"I wanna get off!"

A gruff male voice interrupts a song playing on the speaker and booms, "EVERYONE REMAIN CALM. WE ARE EXPERIENCING SOME TECHNICAL DIFFICULTIES, SO PLEASE SIT TIGHT UNTIL THE FIRE DEPARTMENT COMES TO HELP YOU OUT OF YOUR COMPARTMENT. THANK YOU." I chuckle to myself. The ironic thing is that the town's only fire station is on Main Street and is completely blocked by the carnie rides. They'd have to either call in a fire truck from the closest town to us (which happens to be over 40 miles away) or somehow get a ladder tall enough to reach the highest part of the Ferris wheel out of the firehouse. Knowing my lazy town, they'll have to call in for backup from the next town over.

I'm not mad at all; in fact, I'm thrilled! This gives me an excuse to be up here long enough to enjoy the scenery. To my left I see the Appalachian foothills leading down to our valley; I can almost see the hollers off in the distance. To my right are all the big, fancy East-sider houses. My church sticks out over everything, with a steeple that touches the Heavens. I am so captivated by the view that I hardly notice the huge crowd forming around the ride.

Eventually a fireman on a ladder reaches our box and helps us down. We are the last people off, and, to my disappointment, my parents are there to drive us home.

CHAPTER 12

Danny's Day

Danny meets me and Grandpa around 10:30 in the morning at Dee-Dee's; my Grandpa and I went out for breakfast. We talk about baseball (especially the Yankees), our move to New York, and my birthday.

It is drizzling out but no thunder or anything, just a summer shower. Danny and I ride our bikes through the rain to the actual Valia Springs, and by that I mean the literal fresh water springs in the Jacksons' Holler. From there is a little mountain stream a short ways away with lots of fish. It's a perfect day for fishing, which is exactly what we're gonna do.

We sit on the bank for what seems like hours, just us, the fish, and the silence of the holler. Everything is lush and vibrantly green, and the plunking sound the raindrops make as they smack the surface of the creek is very calming. I've always loved the rain: the feel of it, the smell of it, the way it makes everything look fresh and clean. I kick my shoes and socks off to dip my feet in the tinted-green water, casting the line as far as I can just to see if mine can go farther than Danny's.

Danny is such a quiet boy, he doesn't say anything unless spoken to. I find myself trying to fill the silence with random rambling about stupid things like school and the weather. Danny responds to all my dumb questions with one-syllable, monotone answers. I've gotten two words out of him that were more than one syllable: "Neat-o" and "nifty", both of which (I'm assuming) were supposed to be exclamations he uttered when I started to drone on about my birthday party plans.

I jump at every little noise because the old Jacksons' place, which is right down the road, is supposedly haunted. It's been abandoned for 50 years or something, and it's said that Old Man Jackson was murdered by bandits in the house. We had to pass the house while we were coming up to fish, and believe me, the place looks like something out of a horror movie: broken shutters hanging crazily on their hinges, glass windows with giant chipped holes in them, the roof drooping over the porch, the old wooden door banging open whenever the wind blows through the holler, shingles lying in patches all over the yard, even an old dead sycamore tree that looks like if lighting were to strike it, it would take out the whole house.

You see, the Jacksons founded this town in 1850 when they made money off of oil in the mountains. They found these springs and set up their property nearby. Well, they had a lot of money because of the oil and that's why they chose a little place in Nowhereville, Georgia, so robbers wouldn't come after their fortune.

But Old Man Jackson and his wife lost all six children to cholera. Eventually Mrs. Jackson died and the old man went crazy on his own – thought thunder was gunshots and the rattling windows or creaks and moans of the house was somebody breaking in. He even got himself a guard dog – not to mention he had hallucinations of people in his bedroom!

Anyway, the story is that he used to lock every window and door in his house every night, and he would keep his dog in the front room where the front door is. So one night bandits smashed his bedroom window and shot him, and his dog couldn't do anything but bark because he was locked out of the bedroom. The bandits stole every penny of Old Man Jackson's fortune, which was underneath the bedroom floorboards (he never trusted the bank). No one except bored teenagers from our town dare to go down to the property, Heaven forbid the house.

After a couple of hours we go home, Danny with two catfish and me with one carp. The sun has finally made its debut today and a rainbow begins to appear as we pedal back to my house, where Grandma and Grandpa are going to make a delicious fish casserole. Danny's staying for dinner because his parents (his father's a doctor, his mother's a nurse) are working the night shift at the hospital in Atlanta, which is about a two hour drive from our town. Danny has dinner with us occasionally, but when both his parents are working the night shift he stays the night at one of the boys' houses. Tonight he's staying at Mickey's.

Dinner is excellent. We finish a leisurely day by listening to the Yankee's game on our porch in the lazy, muggy air. Perfect.

CHAPTER 13

Jack's Day

By now, almost my entire house is in boxes in the garage. We finally sold the house to some family from Wisconsin, who is coming to start setting up sometime next week. Oh yeah, and did I mention I only have 20 days left to be with my best friends in the universe before I leave them, most likely forever, and all I'll have left is photographs and memories of a joyous past life? My mother believes I'm overreacting, and maybe I am, but I don't have enough time to worry about that on top of everything else. All I can say is thank the Lord God Almighty for Grandpa. He's making the moving process so much more bearable.

Jack picks me up around 9:40pm because tonight we're going to a late-night movie at the drive-in theater, although, obviously, we're not using a car. Apparently the movie is a surprise, because Jack won't tell me what we're seeing. We walk together to where the theater is; it's at this little gravel lot behind the public high school. When we get there it's pretty crowded, but mostly with older teenagers on dates in their cars and some young married couples from around town. I think Ricky and

Penny are even here somewhere, but it's too dark to tell the cars apart.

We get in the very front, where most of the cars are parked, and Jack goes to get some snacks for us. We decided to split some popcorn but we'll each have our own soda. I lay down the blanket I brought with me for us to sit on, thinking about how it's a little awkward that this seems to be a couples' movie and I'm here with *Jack* of all people. Don't get me wrong, he's nice and all, it's just that he's a bit…odd. I hope that I won't be too uncomfortable watching the movie with him.

He comes back and I shove the thought from my mind, concentrating on the movie. It's cloudy tonight, so the valley is darker than usual. The light from the projection screen illuminates the theater, and the movie begins. It opens to the credits, where it is shortly revealed that the title of the movie is "The Seven Year Itch." I've heard about this movie, and believe me, if Mother found out this is what I'm watching, she'd kill me. The basic storyline is about how this man sends his wife and son up north for the summer and commits adultery with a young lady who lives in the apartment above him. And of course, this young lady is played by none other than Marilyn Monroe. Thankfully, the worst thing that happens is the married man and the young woman kiss (a few times), but still, why does the man feel the need to cheat on his wife? It makes no sense to me. And what's the big deal with the whole 'seven-year' theory? My parents have been married for almost sixteen years and they've never had that sort of problem. When I get married I sure doubt I'll have that kind of problem with my husband, especially if that husband is someone like…wait a second, I am *not* going there. There's no way I could marry him, considering I'm leaving here forever. There's plenty of other fish in the sea, right?

I'm at the part in the movie where the main character is at a therapy session when I notice that Jack, who's been sitting next to me on the picnic blanket the whole time, slowly gets closer and closer next to me. I try to focus on the movie when Jack stretches him arm all casual-like and slips it around my shoulders.

"Do you need some room to stretch your arms?" I ask him uncomfortably.

"No, I'm fine," he says.

"Are you cold, then?" I question, gingerly pulling his arm off of me.

"No, really, I'm okay," he responds.

Later on, when the leading male actor and Marilyn Monroe are walking out from the movie theater together, he does it again. This time I shove his arm roughly and say loudly, "What the *heck* are you DOING?!" He blinks at me.

"Don't you get it? Don't you understand what I've been trying to tell you for the past seven years?" he exclaims and looks me square in the eye. I'm shocked because this is not Jack's usual behavior, so I silently shake my head no. He gulps and grabs my shoulders, still staring intently at me. "Look, I'm sorry, but I can't hide it any longer: I *love* you, Charley!" My jaw literally drops, but he continues, "I probably should've told you sooner, but since you're leaving soon I had to tell you my feelings. I've loved you since the moment I met you, and now you're being yanked from my grasp. I can't lose you. I *can't*! You're the only one I've ever felt this way about!" He's jumped to his feet now and is shouting, while cars are honking and people are hollering for him to get out from in front of the screen. His shadow is blocking half of the projection and he's waving his arms wildly around. Quite honestly, he's scaring the crap out of me. I don't know what to do but gape in horror and humiliation as he turns this into a huge scene.

"Now before you leave, kiss me! Just once! It doesn't have to be long! Or even on the lips! I need something physical to remember you by!"

"What is *WRONG* with you?!?!" I cry as I jump up. Before I know it, he's pulled me in much too close for comfort and is about to forcefully press his mouth to mine when I haul off and punch him square across the face. He reels back and cries, "HOLY S##T!" Once he regains his balance he glares at me with hurt and anger radiating from his face. Then he takes off running. And you know what? I don't even feel that sorry. I just experienced one of the most mortifying moments of my life, Jack will probably never talk to me again, this juicy occurrence will be all over town by tomorrow morning, and my mother's going to find out that I went to a movie she doesn't approve of (not that I really liked it that much, either). What else could possibly go awry? Oh yes, I have to walk home all alone now, which I'm not allowed to do at night (of course because of the junkyard incident). I am dead meat. But on the bright side, Jack doesn't like me anymore! That's a relief in itself.

CHAPTER 14

Mickey's Day

I'm sitting in the living room, smoothing out the last wrinkles of my putrid magenta dress, getting ready for Church as usual on Sunday mornings, when I hear a knock on the front door. Curious as to whom this visitor could be, I peek out the big picture window onto the front porch, where Mickey stands waiting. I dash to the door before Mother can get there. Upon opening it, Mickey crinkles his nose up and frowns at my attire.

"What's with the getup?" he asks gruffly.

"It's Sunday...oh, jeez, don't tell me, it's your day to spend with me, isn't it?" I huff.

"Well for gosh sakes, if I'm so terrible to spend one day with, then what am I still hangin' around here for?" he cracks a smile.

"It's not you! Trust me, I mean, I would *much* rather hang out with you today, but...I have to go to Mass this morning." The only reason why this is an issue is because Mickey is a member of one of the only families in town that doesn't go to Church ever. So normally I would invite him to come with me and my family, but under the circumstances I just stated, I doubt taking him to Mass for the first time in his life would be a good idea.

"Hey, it's no big deal, just explain to your parents that you'd rather go to the pool with me today than go to that ole stuffy barn for the ten thousandth consecutive Sunday." I think he means this as a joke, but if you were in my position you wouldn't be taking that comment very lightly. Missing a single Mass in my house is extraordinarily rare – no, more like *unheard of* – so believe me when I say that waltzing up (to my mother, of all people) and stating that I will be skipping Church to go somewhere of much less importance will guarantee being grounded for at least a week and extra chores on top of the usual amount. I will admit, though, that Mother has been much more lax about her punishments for me so far this summer; maybe it's because she knows how upset I am about moving, and she actually feels sympathy for me. Or maybe it's Grandma and Grandpa, because with them around she feels the need to be less harsh to me. Whatever the case, I am still positive that I will be unable to join Mickey in his plans for today, so I suppose it will be necessary to reschedule.

"I'm really sorry Mick, but I just can't. I'm sorry."

"Well what about *after* Church?"

"I have the Sunday Night Supper to prepare for. It's at our house again this week."

"Well maybe *I* can convince your parents to let you have some fun for once in your life! C'mon, just ask them."

"No. I guarantee if I ask them they'll tell me that I can't."

"Fine. If you won't ask them, then I will." And before I really can figure out what's about to happen, he pushes past me and barges into my house. He clomps all the way down the hall until he gets to the kitchen, where my mother has appeared in the doorway with my father right behind her. Mickey stops mid-step, looks them in the eyes and says what I'd been dreading he'd say: "Charley's coming with me to the pool right now, whether you like it or not." My mother's eyes get wider than saucers, and you can practically hear her mind screaming, '*How could that child have the NERVE to talk to an adult like that?!*' My father is just standing there in stunned silence. Mother opens her mouth to protest, but right before sound comes out Grandpa bumps his way through the crowded doorway and hurriedly ushers Mickey and me back outside.

"You two better thank your lucky stars I got you out of there before you received the wrath of your parents. Now, I don't like the way you talked to those adults, young man, but I feel it would be best if we stayed out of David's and Judy's hair. They're in enough stress as is. Now Charley, go climb up that trellis into your room and get into your swimsuit as quickly as possible. Don't you disturb your parents," Grandpa states seriously.

I am absolutely elated! I hug Grandpa tight around his stomach and gleefully rush to the front of the house and climb the trellis entwined with flower vines. Once in my room, I quickly get out of that wretched dress and into my navy blue ruche swimsuit. I slide on an old T-shirt and shorts over the top, instinctively reach for my Yankees cap on the bed post only to be disappointed when I remember it's gone, and climb out the window and back down the trellis with a towel slung over my shoulder.

"Ready!" I call excitedly as I get back on the ground. Mickey and Grandpa emerge on the porch steps and we leave as rapidly as possible. I don't want to stick around longer than I need to.

"Wait, Grandpa, you're coming with us?" I question.

"Why, yes I am. I intend to keep an eye on you two. And don't think you'll ever get the opportunity to skip Church again anytime soon," Grandpa scolds playfully.

"Sheesh! I didn't think it was *that* big of a deal," sighs Mickey exasperatedly.

"Ha!" I sarcastically laugh, "you don't know the half of it."

"Well maybe you can explain it to me later, but right now, I just wanna get my bare feet off the scorchin' pavement and into some cool water."

Walking barefoot is rather normal in this town. You'd think everyone would rather wear shoes because the asphalt is so hot in the summer, but considering the fact that the bottoms of our feet have become like leather, tough after years of calluses and exposure to the elements, shoes are no longer necessary.

We get to the pool, which is right outside the public high school, and it's completely deserted (which we expected. *Nobody* goes to the pool on Sunday mornings. It's still open, though, as long as there is at least one adult supervising). Grandpa strides through the gate and settles himself into a lounge chair. He's still wearing his Sunday best, and I don't know how he's surviving in this scalding heat. Once again, it's beyond hot and humid, and to be honest the pool is the only place I want to be right now. I can't even imagine being stuffed into that sweaty old Church like a can of sardines today. The sky is just filled with the intense glare of the sun, and I guarantee I'm going to get badly sunburned today.

Mickey shoves his way through and barrels down the row of chairs right to the diving board. He strips off his shirt and shorts and flings them behind him, revealing his swim suit, steps boldly onto the platform, and prepares to dive. I watch him with amusement as I awkwardly step out of my shorts and pull off my shirt. I feel extremely self-conscious.

"*Lovely* day for a swim, isn't it?" the ear-splitting voice of Heather Honeyduke erupts from behind me. I turn to face her, and there she is, in that same old disgusting pink dress, on the other side of the fence that outlines the perimeter of the town aquatic center, on her way to Mass, with her parents far ahead of her, and without a single one of her minions in sight.

"You're quite right. Care to join me?" I ask, dripping with sarcasm. In my mind I add, "*You could take a long walk off a short diving board.*"

"Good grief, no, I'd rather go through Chinese water torture! Well, I can see you and your boyfriend need some alone time, so I'll just be going now," she utters icily.

"Not so brave without your zealots around, are you?" I respond back in an even colder tone.

"My, my, Charlotte, aren't we just a little too defensive. For goodness sake, take a joke, will you?" she instantly snaps back, but in such an innocently sweet tone that you might actually believe what she just said was true. It takes everything in me not to just go right up to her and sock her in the face. Her eyes shift dangerously over to Mickey, who is staring intensely at her in all her gorgeousness from his perch on the diving board.

"Funny how you're the one in the bathing suit and yet I'm *still* getting more attention than you. I'd tell you that you look pretty in it, but I don't like to lie on Sundays."

"You better shut your pie hole before I make you. You're just jealous because Frankie likes *me* ten THOUSAND times more than he likes *you!*" Immediately I realize the damage I've done. Her blue eyes darken to show the most prominent loathing one human being could have towards another. She blinks rapidly and her eyes shift back to their old wickedly deceitful glaze.

"Oh, *do* forgive me Charlotte. I realize this is a tender topic for you. You're clearly under the delusion that Frankie actually *likes* you." She walks slowly and steadily towards, and then through, the gate to the pool, and makes her way over to me nonchalantly, like a tiger waiting to pounce on its prey. Every warning signal in my whole body is going off, but I can't stop her from coming right up to me and wrapping me in a tight embrace. I've just barely gotten over the shock of having Heather Honeyduke actually *hug* me, when I feel a small tug at the back of my neck, and before I know it, my bathing suit halter top has come untied. I feel the top of my swim suit slide and slip down faster than I can react. Heather jumps back as I desperately try to clutch my body, shielding what is now exposed. She dashes back out the gate and onto the sidewalk, calling, "Au revoir!" and cackling. As she runs away I make a mad grab for my towel and immediately wrap it around my front. Just before she turns the corner, I scream at the top of my lungs, "DON'T LET THE CHURCH DOOR HIT YOU ON THE WAY OUT!!!"

On the verge of tears and more embarrassed than I've ever been in my life, I sprint to the women's changing room, the towel still tightly wound around my body. Once I'm in a stall, I quickly retie my suit, and try to take deep breaths to calm myself. I promised myself the first day of third grade, the day that Heather spilled the water on my lap, that I would NEVER, *EVER* cry over something she or her followers did to me. It's been insanely hard, but once I put my mind to something I always succeed; so far I have come close to, but still I have never, cried over her cruelties. And I'll be damned if I'm gonna start today.

Shaken and mortified, I sheepishly go back outside into the bright, hot sunny day. After that experience, all I really want to do is go sit down and not talk to anybody. I take the open chaise next to Grandpa, lie down, and cover my head with my towel in shame.

"Charley," Grandpa murmurs, "are you alright?" I want to scream, "*No, I'm not 'alright', this whole damn summer hasn't been 'alright'!*" but instead I just sigh in response. "I…I am so, so, *so* sorry that girl did that to you…I just, I don't know what to say…for once your ole granddad is speechless, heheh…"

There's a splashing sound emanating from the pool, and then I hear Mickey sloshing water and hoist himself out. He pads across the concrete to where I'm sitting and plops himself onto the chair next to me.

"If it helps make ya feel better, I didn't see nothin'…" Mickey's voice trails off. I appreciate their kind words, but it doesn't take away the humiliation I just experienced.

"Grandpa, how could jealousy make someone *that* despicable? How?!" I cry.

"I don't know, dear…jealousy, like all sin, comes with a lack of faith. She must not have enough Jesus in her life to fill the hole her jealousy is in."

"Well, I don't know what to do about her! I feel like every year she just gets worse."

"Honey, the only thing you can truly do is pray for her. Pray for her hard and often, and trust God to take care of the rest."

"Mr. Mason, how do you know so much about faith?" Mickey suddenly asks. I pull the towel off my face and sit straight up, shocked. Grandpa looks taken aback.

"Why son, you just sit back and let me tell you a story. You might not believe this, but I was destined to be a priest since the day I was born. My mother had always wanted to be a nun, but she was the oldest sister; back in those days the younger sisters were only allowed to get married after the oldest sister did. She knew her younger sister had already found herself her true love, and my mother did the unselfish thing by giving up her lifelong dream of become a Sister just so her younger sisters could get married. For her entire life, you could tell she wished she was a nun. But she continued her life as one of the most devout women I've ever known. When I was born, she vowed that I, her first son, would be a priest, and in a way fulfill her dreams of a religious life. All throughout my childhood I was told I was going to be a priest, and at the age of 14 is was shipped off to St. Joseph's Seminary in Yonkers, New York. I was all set and ready to be a priest, just like everyone had planned. But then I failed Latin, and I wasn't allowed to enter into the priesthood. My mother took it the hardest; she was so disappointed, she didn't speak a word to me for months. I had no idea where my future was supposed to go. So I did the one thing I knew how to do the best: I prayed. Sure enough, I was drafted by the Yankees for my extraordinary high school baseball career. And as they say, the rest is history."

"Is that why it's so dang important for you and your family to go to Church?"

"Well, it's like this: we ask God to help us and forgive us and bless us and give us things all the time, and all He wants in return is one hour a week just to listen and talk to Him. Doesn't that seem like a pretty fair deal?" Grandpa explains.

"Yeah, I guess so," Mickey replies.

"I sure hope Heather Honeyduke is listening good and hard. Maybe she'll hear the voice of Jesus coming from the Heavens telling her she better start being nicer to people," I frown.

"Ah, if only it were that simple. You have to *want* to listen to God in order to hear anything, and it seems to me that she probably doesn't care all that much one way or another. If she did care, she would be making an effort to treat people more kindly. Now enough serious talk, we're burning daylight! You two go on and have some fun."

I get up and follow Mickey over to the pool. We both jump in, and the refreshing water surrounding my body combined with the sensation of weightlessness make me forget my troubles and just take in the here and now. When I come up for air I smile and everything feels instantly better. I grin at Mickey and my grandpa, true happiness replacing my former degradation. I'm about to go back under, but just before I do I hear my grandfather whisper, "I don't ever want to forget that smile." His eyes are closed, but in my heart I know he's talking about me. And I think to myself, "I don't ever want to forget this moment."

CHAPTER 15

JC's Day

J C picks me up at sunset on his day. This makes Grandpa a little suspicious.

"And where are you taking Charley so late in the evening?" he asks on the porch. JC pulls out two jars and a flashlight.

"We're just gonna go catch us some fireflies is all," he replies. Grandpa nods but still wears a suspecting look. The whole town found out about the episode with Jack, so obviously it made its way back to my family. They've had to double my safety rules for hanging out with the guys, and are totally distrusting if any of them take me someplace after dark. This explains my Grandpa's no-nonsense behavior.

"Well, you better be back by ten with her, young man, or you're in for a world of trouble. You understand me?" Grandpa says very seriously. JC nods quickly, then takes off down the porch steps and gets on his bicycle. I do the same thing, but reassure Grandpa that I'll be fine. I can hear thunder rumbling and rolling off in the distance but I don't really pay it much attention.

Once we're on the road and far enough away from my house, I turn my attention to JC. There's no way he would *ever* forcibly go firefly catching.

"OK, gig's up. Where are we really going?" I ask him.

"To the ole haunted Jackson place. I gotta see if you can spend a half hour by yourself. In. The. *House.*" He says it so dramatically that it makes me laugh.

"Puh-*leeze*, a half hour? Is that all? And what's in it for you?"

"I get you to take something from the house, which I'll show to my brother to prove that I'm worthy enough to join his club," he replies.

"Well what if I don't make it the half hour? What do I lose? And how come you're not going inside with me? It's *your* challenge."

"You'll look like a chicken if you can't make the half hour, but it's not like you'll lose something. And I'm not going inside because I have to time you. Plus if you die my life is more valuable than yours."

"Wow. Thanks for making me feel good about myself," I joke sarcastically. I feel a few raindrops sprinkle on my arms and head, so I glance up to a cloudy, dark sky just as it starts raining cats and dogs. I'm drenched to the bone in seconds. Thunder and lightning quickly follow the downpour. We pedal as fast as we can to the Jackson property, set our bikes on the porch, and both end up coming in the house to stay dry (although the effort was pretty much futile). Water is seeping through the ceiling and there are multiple puddles on the floor. It's so cold, I feel like if there was any light I would be able to see my breath. My heart is pumping a thousand beats per minute and I'm shivering uncontrollably.

I look around. It's almost completely pitch black; the only reason I can see things is because the lightning continually illuminates the house. The place is super creepy: leaky roof, pitch blackness, creaky floorboards, several rotted holes in the structure, and to top it all off there's a thunderstorm. It smells disgustingly earthy and musty.

"Well, it's a good thing I brought my flashlight," JC says quietly, clicking it on. It immediately shuts off. He turns it on again. It blinks and then dies. He hits the 'on' switch, and it doesn't even make so much as a flicker.

"That's odd," he tries to keep his voice from sounding alarmed, "I just put a new battery in it this afternoon." The stormy wind rattles the windows, and the house creaks and moans with the gales.

"W-w-well," JC stutters, "proceed." I gulp and start forward slowly. There's so much lightning I don't think we really need a flashlight. I take a few steps across the threshold, then stop.

"Do you hear that?" I ask. Every hair on the back of my neck is standing straight up, and goosebumps spread down my arms.

"H-hear w-what?"

"Those footsteps, I think they're coming from the attic." We're silent as we listen to the faint *thud, thud, thud* coming from somewhere above us. We keep going, but only out of sheer terror. We get to the kitchen when the shutters start banging. There's a cracking noise, like the splintering of wood, and JC yelps, "OUCH!"

I turn around and his foot is stuck in a hole in the floor. I quickly pull him out.

"Are you alright? Let's go back."

"No, I'm fine. I just gotta see the bedroom where the old guy died." Just then the footsteps start coming from the cellar stairs: *creak, creeeeaaaak, creak.* I swallow back a scream. We race down the hall to the stairway to the second floor. Every step moans and every crack of thunder shakes the house.

The first room we see is the washroom. The tub is covered in rust and grime and the mirror is cracked in the frame.

"This is too weird," JC whispers. We're both over the initial shock of prowling through the haunted house, but we're still terrified out of our minds.

There's a portrait of a beautiful woman with long dark hair hanging above the washbasin. She must've been Mrs. Jackson. Her eyes are sad despite her smile – her expression is like the *Mona Lisa*'s.

We exit the washroom and enter the nursery. It's freezing in there. I get chills up my spine when I see the rocking chair in the corner, as empty as the desert, rocking slowly by itself. I try to turn and leave, but I can't look away. JC yanks me out and we go into the next room. Footsteps start in the attic again. I clutch JC's arm. The bed in this bedroom has the indentation of a sleeping body.

Finally we get to the last door of the hallway, on the very back wall. We enter it after one good twist on the doorknob; but even though the door opens, the knob falls off. JC picks it up and puts it in his pocket. I guess this is the proof that he's going to give his brother that he actually went inside the house. The door closes by itself and shuts – tight. A gust of wind blows through the spot where the glass is shattered in the window. JC jumps back.

"I just stepped on something!" he exclaims. I peer through the darkness at the pile of broken glass, glinting in the thunderbolts' glow. My eyes rove the ground. I spy a shotgun, just lying there, shining wood handle and rusty barrel. This is just *too* weird.

Then, with a flash of lightning, I scream at the top of my lungs, but it's drowned out by the rolling thunder. Lying dead right next to the bed is the skeletal corpse of Old Man Jackson. I grab JC by the wrist and turn to slam the door open when I hear the sharp but distant howl of an ancient guard dog. There's a gigantic CRACK from outside, and then the old sycamore tree starts to tip over onto the house. I ram into the door with all my might, and it finally bursts open just as the ceiling starts to cave in from the weight of the tree. We run out of there so fast we could've set an Olympic record: down the hall, down the stairs, through the kitchen, parlor, living room, and foyer, out the door, on the porch, on our bikes and pedaling as fast as physically possible, all the while adrenaline pulsing through us as we narrowly escape the collapsing structure. We don't even consider stopping until we get to my street. Soaked through and through, out of breath, and covered in mud, I stop to breathe after completely hyperventilating for the entire bike ride.

Suddenly all the fear, exhaustion, and lack of oxygen catch up to me, and I faint. Again. Right there in front of JC.

CHAPTER 16

Frankie's Story

"Are we gonna get her parents?" someone asks quietly.

"No, just wait a few minutes. She'll come-to," someone else replies. I blink and look around. I'm lying on the couch in Frankie's living room; both he and JC are staring down at me. I sit up.

"How long was I out this time?" I ask, rubbing my head.

"Only 'bout five minutes," JC responds.

"Here, take some water," Frankie hands me a cup. I sip gratefully. "Are you okay, Charley?" he looks concerned. "That's quite a bump you got there, JC told me you hit the pavement pretty hard. You don't got a concussion, do you?"

"No, I'm fine. Really! It's just that I was scared and out of breath." I reach up to rub my fingers over the lump forming on my forehead, and Frankie gently takes my hand away so he can put an ice-filled washcloth on the spot.

"Why were you scared? JC, *what* did you do this time?"

"Well, it all started because I wanted to join my older brother's club, you see, and I kinda had to go into the old Jackson house, and I figured that Charley wouldn't mind–"

"You took her inside the *house*?!"

"Well, yeah, but it's not as bad as it sounds–"

"It sounds pretty bad to begin with! Loads of things could go wrong! You should've thought about this before you went and –"

"Guys! Really!" I interrupt, "I'm OK! In fact, I'm better than OK! I'm great! You don't need to start an argument over my well-being. I can take care of myself." The two boys get all quiet.

"Hey, where's your dad?" JC asks Frankie out of nowhere.

"He's helpin' my uncle at the restaurant." The two of them exchange glances, then JC says slowly, "I'm gonna go home now." He walks out the front door and leaves.

"You sure you're OK?"

"Yes, I'm sure!" I cry. There's a long awkward silence.

"I'm sorry. I tend to overreact when someone I care about is in trouble or gets hurt. It's because… because of my mother." My eyes widen. This is the first time Frankie's really talked about his mother to me. It's sort-of an untouchable subject between us.

"You've probably heard the story from one of the ladies around town. I was almost eight and Ricky was twelve. My brother, dad, and I were going fishing. My mother was at her friend's house for the afternoon. When we finally got home, Mom's friend's husband was waiting for us. He told us that my mother had collapsed a few hours earlier and was rushed to the nearest hospital. Apparently she'd had a brain tumor. She hung on for weeks after that, clinging to life in a hospital room. One night we got a phone call from the hospital. And just like *that*," he snaps his fingers for emphasis, "she was gone." His gaze is distant. I feel bad that he even brought it up. I squeeze his hand in a pathetic attempt to make him feel better.

"I'll see you tomorrow," I murmur. I leave and cross the street, and can't help realizing my bike is already parked in my garage. JC probably did that…

Then it hits me. Frankie was the one who carried me both times I fainted.

CHAPTER 17

Arthur's Day

I t's a clear, beautiful night, warm but not too warm. Arthur and I are out on the hill behind the baseball diamond.

"Tonight, we stargaze," Arthur smiles as he sets up his telescope. My parents have extended my curfew tonight because A) my father loaded the telescope we're using into Grandpa's truck bed, drove it to the hill and helped us set it up, proving that Arthur and I are going to do what we claimed we would do, and B) they don't think Arthur will try to "pull any stunts like the redheaded boy did". And they're right in their assumptions. Out of all the guys, Arthur's probably the nicest (even if he is kind of an egghead).

We're using our star chart to search for Sagittarius when Arthur asks, "So. Do you like anybody?" just as casual as asking what the weather's like. I was taken aback.

"Why do you ask?" I question him.

"I dunno. Just wonderin'."

"Well I don't like anybody at my school, if that's what you mean, and I DO NOT like Jack, if *that's* what you mean."

"Oh no, I knew that already. I was just wonderin' if you like someone like Larry...or JC...or, and I'm just spitballing here, maybe Frankie...?"

My face turns bright red, and even with his glasses to the telescope lens I can tell he knows he got me.

"OK, and I'm not saying I do, but if hypothetically speaking I did on the slightest chance like Larry or JC or Frankie or even you, how could you tell?"

"Because they are – excuse me, *would be* – the person you spend the most time with."

"Oh baloney! I spend an equal amount of time with everybody – that's the whole point of this 'every guy gets his own day' thing."

"OK, fine, but you still do – I mean *would* – look at him in that admiring way with that shine in your eyes."

"Oh, you don't know beans! It seems like someone's been paying a little *too* much attention to me," I retort.

"What? You think I – I mean I was only – you know what? I don't know what you mean – you're reading too much into this. I was only suggesting something because

I was told to," he sputters in a very flustered way. I'm sick of trying to dodge the bullet, so I decide to give him what he wants (even if that means lying).

"Alright, I admit it! I like JC. There. Ya happy now?" His smug grin at finally getting an answer turns into a scowl.

"Aw, quit lyin'! Everyone knows you like Frankie, so why don't you just admit it?"

"I'll admit it as soon as he admits that *he* likes *me!*" I cry. Well that seems to shut him up. There's an awkward silence as I take my turn looking for the Big and Little Dippers.

"I'm sorry I brought that up. We don't have to talk about it if you don't want to," he apologizes. Then he adds, "But hypothetically speaking, if he *did* like you, would you like him?"

Something told me I didn't have to respond, because it was pretty obvious he knew the answer. I sighed.

"I'll take that as a yes."

CHAPTER 18

Happy Birthday

The morning of July 29th, 1955 is a wonderful way to start my birthday.

I awaken to the mouthwatering aroma of Grandma's peach pie. I sit up in bed, yawn, stretch and go downstairs into the kitchen. Father, Mother, Ginger, Grandma, and Grandpa are all there, sitting at the table (except for Ginger, who's sitting *under* the table) with a huge stack of blackberry and raspberry flapjacks.

"You guys are the best!" I cry as I hug everyone.

That afternoon, Father and I are setting up for my backyard barbecue/birthday party when three strange people let themselves into our backyard and waltz right up to me.

"Happy Birthday!" a man, woman, and girl, who all have the same orange hair, freckles, and spectacles that could rival only Arthur's glasses, exclaim in unison. I stare blankly at them; I've honestly never seen them in my life, and believe me, they're not the kind of people you easily forget.

"I'm Sheila, this is Mark, and Petunia is our daughter. We're the McDougals from Wisconsin. We can't *wait* to move into our new home!" the woman smiles enthusiastically (and, to be honest, a little bit crazily). *Now* I understand – they're the people who bought my house.

"Hi. I'm Petunia. I'm gonna be fifteen next month," she squeaks in her nasally, congested voice. She's the skinniest girl I've ever seen, I've got two inches on her, *and* she has dental headgear. Her hair is in curly pigtails on either side of her head. Her glasses are super thick with boxy, black frames. Her eyes are a moss green.

She hands me a box. "We got you a birthday present, Charlotte," she explains, and at the same time spits all over me. She's obviously a mouth-breather with some serious salivation issues. Not to mention it kind of scares me how she already knows my name.

Just then the whole team enters my backyard in a large cluster.

"Oh my gosh! There's SO MANY *BOYS*!" Petunia squeals. "Who's that handsome fella over there?" she points near the picnic table. I almost gag.

"Y-y-you mean the tall, tan boy in the striped shirt?" I stutter.

"No, silly! The super cutie next to him." She smiles mischievously and flirtatiously, raising her eyebrows multiple times for emphasis as she twirls one of her pigtails. I almost gag again, but for a different reason.

"You mean JACK?!?" I keep myself from laughing hysterically out loud.

"Yeah, why? He's not taken is he!?" she sounds desperately alarmed.

"Oh, *gosh*, no! He's ALL yours." She smiles that flirty grin again.

"Well it was nice meeting you," she says absently, then strolls right over to him. Arthur sneaks up behind me after she leaves.

"So who was that?" he raises his eyebrows. I turn to him.

"Just your new neighbor, Petunia McDougal."

"Hmm. Does *she* like Frankie, too?" he asks with a sly smile.

"No, she likes Jack, of all people. Why do you ask?"

"I was just gonna tell her she'd have to wait in line with pretty much every other girl in our age group."

"Is that supposed to make me jealous?"

"Hypothetically speaking: if it was, it's working." I blush deep red. Arthur can be such a jerk (but in a good way).

We look back at Jack and Petunia, who are now gazing all lovey-dovey into each others' eyes. Jack's fluffing his shirt collar and Petunia's twirling her pigtail again. It's enough to make you puke.

Well, it's a beautiful afternoon: clear blue sky, 76 degrees with a nice breeze. Not a cloud in sight.

Everyone crowds around the old maple tree in my backyard (everyone, that is, except Petunia and Jack, who are secretly making out in the garage) to listen to nine innings of the Yankees kicking the Kansas City Athletics' butts.

Mother doesn't really care about baseball, but she listens to show she supports my passion. At least Grandma has grown to love it; "You can't expect to marry a professional baseball player and never enjoy the sport," is what she always says. Grandpa got her tickets to every single one of his games and his love for baseball finally rubbed off on her.

When the game ends it's time for dinner. I'm just about to sit down next to Frankie at the dinner table when our obnoxiously loud doorbell chimes twice.

"Can you get that, honey?" Mother asks, but I know it's really not a question; it's a command. I go answer the front door and who should be standing there but the Pretty Posse.

"Hi," Anne speaks, "we're here for your birthday party." She says it so slowly you'd think I don't understand English.

"The shindig's around back," I sigh. They follow me to the gate at the side of the house that leads to the backyard.

"Oh. Well isn't this just...quaint," winces Sarah. Mary flings a small box into my hands.

"Here's your gift," she grimaces, "it from all of us."

"Now if you don't mind, we're going to thank your mother for inviting us," Ella glowers.

They're all wearing the usual dresses, just like at the Sunday Night Suppers. I guess my mother failed to inform them that this is a casual occasion. I almost feel bad for them, but then again, they actually like wearing the dumb dresses. It's their own fault that they'll stick out like sore thumbs here.

Sophie suddenly stops. "Girls, look!" she exclaims, "Charlotte's invited her *boy*friends!" she throws her head back and cackles.

Catherine gasps. "I don't *believe* it!" she murmurs. The other girls turn and ask, "What ever could it be, Cathy?" in unison, as if it *literally* was rehearsed.

"How in the world did *Charlotte Mason* get *Frankie Deluccio* to come to her party?" she cries. The girls erupt in whispering until Heather Honeyduke, who is at her usual place in the center of the pack of gossiping girls, strides over and takes the only spot left at the picnic table, right next to Frankie. In other words, She. Took. My. *Seat.* The other girls giggle in excitement at the fact that their beloved queen is sitting next to the most handsome boy in Valia Springs.

"Charlotte, *do* tell us how *he* actually came. Did you threaten him with a knife to his throat or a gun to his head?" Mary scoffs.

"Neither, actually; he's just my neighbor, that's all. We've only been best friends since I moved here," I answer sarcastically.

"*You're* best friends with *Frankie Deluccio*?! How did *that* happen?" Ella asks suspiciously, as if I were lying. I just roll my eyes.

Well, I'm hungry, so like any normal person, I just go up to Heather and simply ask as nice as humanly possible, "May I please have my seat back?" I even add a huge, phony grin to top it all off. I hope my sugary sweetness might get her to be generous for once in her life.

"There are plenty of other seats at this table, don't you think?" she replies, dripping with her own batch of sugary sweetness.

"But –," I start, but Mother shoots me the 'be nice' warning look. I just accept this and squeeze between Arthur and Petunia.

Heather and her clones insist that "we're genuinely not hungry, and simply *couldn't* make pigs of ourselves," with a direct glance at me gnawing into a large piece of steak. I can't help but notice how much flirting Heather does, tossing her golden hair this way and that, batting her eyelashes, and giggling girlishly at every single thing Frankie utters, until it's time for cake. Well, in this case, pie.

Grandma brings out her peach pie with fifteen candles aglow along the rim. Everybody sings "Happy Birthday" and I blow out the candles in one breath. I make the same wish every year; that I'll play for the Yankees with Frankie.

Finally after every last crumb has been eaten it's time to open presents. The first one I open is from the Pretty Posse. It's a rosary.

"How lovely," I fake smile. That thing will be donated or sold as soon as we move. I already have three rosaries as is. "Thanks, girls," I say to them, and they all look like they couldn't possibly care less.

The next present I open is the little box Petunia gave me. It contains a pair of pearl earrings. Yuck. My ears aren't pierced anyway, so these will probably be given away soon too.

"How thoughtful," I say kindly to the McDougals. Next, my parents bring out a big box from the garage.

"Be gentle when you open it," Mother warns as I tear off the wrapping paper and rip open the box lid. Inside, staring up at me, is the most adorable beagle puppy.

"Awww," everyone coos.

"It's a boy," Father tells me.

"What're ya gonna name it?" Max asks. I think about it for a while, then, finally I decide on something.

"Yank. Like short for Yankee." I take Yank out of the box and hug him. Ginger trots over from her shady spot under a chair. I set him down by Ginger and they sniff each other.

"He's sooo cute," Anne grins. The two dogs curl up next to each other in the box, which they tipped on its side. Who knew a dachshund and beagle could be best friends?

"Open ours next!" Larry exclaims. The team's gift is an envelope – or at least whatever's inside it. There's a piece of paper tucked inside that reads: "*To our best friend Charley. We won't forget or replace you. Hope you have a great last summer. ~The Team*". The paper has all of their signatures on it. I'm about to drop the envelope when I notice two thin strips of paper enclosed. I take them out and scream in happiness; they're tickets to a Yankees game!

"Oh my gosh! I can't believe it! How did you get them?!" I exclaim, and before I know it, tears are welling in my eyes. I give each of the guys a hug.

"We've been savin' our money since the beginning of summer cuz we wanted to get you something good this year. We only had enough money for two tickets, and they're not the best seats, but we knew you'd like 'em anyway," Danny explains, "they arrived in the mail three days ago. The game ain't til Labor Day, so you got some time." Wow. I've never heard Danny say so many words together at one time! Ha, I'm just glad I got to hear it before I leave Valia Springs.

"I can't wait!!!" I turn to Grandpa. "Will you take me? *Please*?" I beg.

"Well I suppose…if I'm feeling up to it…" he replies uncertainly.

Out of nowhere, we hear a car pulling up to my house and a black sedan coasts into our driveway. Grandpa smiles.

"Your present's here, Charley," he says satisfactorily. He walks over to the fancy black car and out comes a man about five-foot-eight, who's muscular, wearing sunglasses, a baseball cap, and is holding *my* Yankees hat! But to my joy the entire white part of the cap is covered in autographs. The mysterious stranger hands it to me.

"The entire 1955 Yankees team signed this," he tells me, his voice low and deep. My team crowds around me to get a good look at it. Everything except the blue NY logo is written on. This is the best gift I've ever gotten!

"Thank you, stranger," I say in awe as I shake his hand.

"You don't have to call me a stranger," he says as he takes off the sunglasses, "cuz most people call me Yogi." My jaw drops. I just shook hands with Yogi Berra!!! Could this day get any better?!

"Oh my gosh! This is so amazing to meet you!"

"So Charley...it is Charley, right?" I nod. "Your granddad tells me you and a friend of yours want to make it to the Major Leagues. Am I right?"

"Yeah," I nod, "me and Frankie here," (I nudge Frankie, who's gaping) "have been dreaming of playing for the Yankees together for eight years. Frankie's one of your biggest fans." I don't mention that Frankie likes Mickey Mantle a tiny bit better because I don't want to offend Mr. Berra.

"Well when you're old enough I'll put in a good word for you," Yogi tells Frankie. Now it makes sense why Berra wasn't in the game today; he probably flew to Atlanta early this morning and spent the whole day trying to get here.

"Why don't you come and sit down," Grandpa pulls over a chair for him. I fetch him a glass of lemonade from the pitcher on the picnic table.

Frankie says to me, "I'm gonna get my lucky bat for him to sign," and jogs out of my yard. Too bad Heather is close behind him. I grit my teeth in frustration at that darn girl. She just gets on my last nerve.

All the other girls and boys sit down around Yogi Berra as he tells us a story about his first game in the majors. In a comical way, it reminds me of little children gathering around the Santa Claus that's at the mall during December for story time. The boys all have that same sort of wonder on their faces as they get lost in the tales presented to them by a jolly old ballplayer.

Frankie's back a few minutes later with Heather at his side. He's got his bat and a permanent marker.

"Mr. Berra, will you autograph this bat for me?" he asks sheepishly.

"Sure kid," Yogi replies, and makes his signature really bold.

"Wow, Frankie. You're *sooo* lucky this baseball player signed your bat for you. My daddy knows a lot of other professional baseball players, if you want to meet them…" she bats her eyelashes at him.

"Excuse me Heather, but I gotta use the can," he frowns.

"Remember to lock the door Frankie. Heather might follow you in!" JC calls. Heather glares at him.

"Shut up!" she growls. JC cracks his knuckles in an intimidating way.

"Oh don't act so tough. You wouldn't hurt a girl, *would* you?" she asks menacingly. He raises his eyebrows as if to say, 'you're right…at least not while witnesses are around.' I worry about that kid sometimes.

Yogi Berra is cracking up while telling a story to our group. The other guys are listening intently, and normally I would be, too, but right now I'm really distracted.

Arthur comes and sits next to me in a shady corner of the yard.

"I'm a little worried. Frankie's been gone a while," I whisper to him.

"Don't worry," he whispers back, "he's just hiding in the gap between your garage and the fence. But now do you see what I mean about how girls hafta get in line for him?" I nod knowingly.

"She's awfully pretty, though. Heather's got the most gorgeous blonde hair in town. She's Penny's younger sister for cryin' out loud!"

"Yeah, she *is* pretty," Arthur admits, "but guys usually aren't attracted to girls who stalk them. And besides, Frankie likes *you*. He always has and probably always will." I can't help but smile bashfully at this wonderful, yet strangely not surprising, news. My stomach fills with butterflies and I'm giddy with joy.

"You're the best, Arthur," I say as I hug him.

"I know," he replies.

≈

I sneak to Frankie's hiding place as soon as Heather's not looking.

"Hi," I say quietly. He jumps.

"Thank God it's you. I thought it was Heather again. She's been following me everywhere."

"I noticed."

"I've barely talked to you at all today. Are you having a good party?"

"Yeah, except for the Pretty Posse, but it's so amazing that Yogi Berra came."

"I know. You are so lucky."

"It's just good to finally be alone," I sigh. The sun is setting. It's getting dark. I lean in, and so does he, and I lift my head up to meet his face…

"Hey, Heather! I FOUND HIM!" Mary yells at the top of her lungs. Frankie says a very bad Italian swear word under his breath. I know what it means because Arthur told me once. Don't even ask how *he* knows the definition.

Heather comes running up.

"Wanna dance?" she grabs his hand and pulls him to the lawn near the radio. Someone has turned it to the Modern Music station. Something by Frank Sinatra is playing as I follow them out and watch them dance. Cathy and Sophie are the only girls not dancing.

"Charlotte, we have to talk. In the house. Now," Sophie commands. I'm positive I smell a rat, but I lead them through the back door into the kitchen, jealousy and rage burning inside me as I think of Heather dancing with Frankie. *Heather 2, Charlotte -3.*

"This isn't private enough. Is there a large closet or bathroom we could go in?" Cathy suggests. I nod and, though I feel like something fishy is going on here, lead them to the first floor bathroom. I step inside and turn to the girls.

"Sorry Charlotte, but Heather's making us do this!" Cathy apologizes genuinely (I can see the true remorse in her eyes), and the two girls slam the bathroom door closed. I try to turn the knob, but the door handle is just *not* twisting. I lean on the door with my shoulder and shove as hard as possible. The only progress I make is forming a bruise on my upper arm. I can't believe those little witches locked me in here! Well, I actually can believe it, but still! How do they have the nerve to do something like this?

I scramble over to the bathroom window above the toilet, and clamber on top of the closed lid to see outside. I spy Heather and Frankie still dancing, and I realize why the girls trapped me in here. Heather didn't want her only opportunity to ever dance with Frankie ruined. I slide open the window, planning to climb out, when I spot Mickey. He's sitting alone below the window at the picnic table.

"Mickey!" I call to him. He turns and looks around. "Up here!" I bang on the glass. He sees me.

"What's wrong?" he looks confused.

"I'm locked in here! Come get me out!" I cry.

"Alright, I'm comin'," he replies reassuringly. I hear him open the back door and come trotting through the house, looking for the correct room. I pound on the door so he'll find me quicker.

"OK Charley, I'm gonna try to get you out of there," I hear Mickey say from the other side of the door. I can hear the radio that's out in the backyard through the open window. "Making Believe" by Kitty Wells is starting to play, and the first few notes drift into the claustrophobic lavatory. It's one of the most popular songs among my peer group in this town, and Heather must be absolutely giddy with happiness that she's dancing to it with Frankie while I'm out of her way, stuck in a bathroom. I feel like I want to cry because everyone's having a good time without me, and that dog-gone sappy song isn't helping to lighten the mood.

"Um...Charley, there's a chair that's jamming the door closed...but the doorknob is stuck between the wooden slats that make up the back of the chair...and I can't get the chair to come off," Mickey informs me. "I'd have to get a screwdriver to take off the doorknob completely." My heart sinks with disappointment.

"I don't even know if we have a screwdriver," I tell him, "the only other way out is to jump out the window."

It sounds quite ridiculous, not to mention a bit extreme, to jump out the window, but it's not too high off the ground and I bet I can just manage to squeeze through.

"Well, it's worth a try," Mickey admits. "I'll meet you outside, then." I go back to the window and peer outside. Almost everyone here is dancing, even my parents, not to mention Jack and Petunia are practically having the time of their lives just holding onto each other. That Kitty Wells song is still playing, but it'll end in less than a minute. Determined to have a dance with Frankie, I swing my legs out the window and push myself off the ledge. I land on my hands and knees on the grass below. The thud of my weight hitting the ground causes a lot of my guests to turn and stare at me. Quickly standing, I rush up to Heather and tap on her shoulder.

"Who let *you* out of the closet?" she sneers, but I ignore her.

"May I cut in?" I ask impatiently, not even waiting for an answer. Frankie grabs my hands and we twirl off into the darkest corner where the radio is. Evening has spread and it's already starting to get dark. Dancing in the shade of the tree just adds to the black of the oncoming night.

"I love this song," I say quietly. I'm just soaking in the bliss of dancing on my birthday with the boy I've always dreamed of dancing with, when the song tragically ends. It was a short moment of pure joy, but *completely* worth jumping out a window for.

BEEEEEP!!! A car horn shatters the quiet night. Yogi Berra honks his horn as he pulls out of the driveway. Gradually everyone leaves. My fifteenth birthday is nearly gone, only two hours left. I failed at my third attempted first kiss so far in two months, and yet it took Petunia all of two minutes to get Jack to kiss her (how that is even possible, I have no clue. She has HEADGEAR, for Heaven's sake!). The only good thing about moving is never seeing Heather or the Pretty Posse ever again.

CHAPTER 19

Bella Notte

On the evening of July 31st, 1955 Frankie Deluccio picks me up at 9:30pm. My family decided my curfew could be 11:15 tonight, and I was lent a watch that would chime on the hour, to remind me at 11:00 that it would be time to start heading home.

When Frankie picks me up he's wearing a suit. I feel very out of place because I'm just in some old shorts and a T-shirt.

"Are we going somewhere fancy?" I ask him. He smiles mysteriously and replies, "It's a surprise. That's why I want you to wear this blindfold." I'll admit I'm a bit puzzled, but definitely in a good way.

I go along with it; I keep my eyes shut tight while he guides me toward whatever this surprise is. With one hand on my left shoulder and another holding onto my left hand, he leads me to wherever our destination is. I have absolutely no idea where we're going, but wherever it is, it's taking quite a while to walk there. Finally we stop and Frankie says, "Open your eyes."

I take off the blindfold and immediately know I'm in the rich neighborhood, the East Side. I looked up at a sign that reads, "Salvatore Anetrini's Fine Italian Restaurant". I smile. It smells like fresh-baked lasagna, basil, cheese, and wine. Inside, Dean Martin's "That's Amore" is drifting out the open front door.

"The place is deserted," I state.

"That's because my uncle reserved the entire place just for us," he grins and takes me by the hand. We go inside and I choose a nice two-person table in the back. We sit down and Frankie's aunt comes over to pour us some grape juice. She puts a basket of breadsticks on the table and some olive oil dip.

"What would you like for dinner?" she asks in her slight Italian accent.

"Spaghetti, please," I smile. She leaves and goes into the kitchen. "You didn't order anything," I say to Frankie.

"I know, just wait. Aunt Viviana knows what to do," he replies. We munch on breadsticks for a while and talk about baseball, my party, and, especially, Heather Honeyduke.

"How can someone so mean be related to Penny?" I wonder aloud.

"I don't know! I was wondering the same thing," Frankie exclaims.

"You know, she had her two henchgirls lock me in the bathroom at my party so I couldn't interfere with you and her dancing."

"That's awful! I can't believe anyone would do something like that."

"Yeah, well, you don't know the girls at my school like I do."

"Guess what? She tried to kiss me at my house when I went to get my bat. And she tried to kiss me *again* while we were dancing."

"Seriously?"

"Seriously. She's crazy."

"Crazy *and* gorgeous. Those qualities combined can be lethal."

"And did you see Jack and that girl Petunia? They were looking at each other so...weird...it made me nauseous," he laughs.

"I know, right? They were kissing the entire time we listened to the game. They're a match made in Heaven in every sense of the word."

"I always knew Jack had a soulmate. I just didn't know who the poor, unlucky soul was. But it makes sense about them making out in the garage. It makes me think of the time he tried to make a move on you at the movie."

"Don't remind me," I sigh. Just then Aunt Viviana comes out with a single large spaghetti platter topped with Parmesan cheese and meatballs. She puts it on the table along with two forks.

"Enjoy," she smiles. When she walks away I question, "But there's only one plate. Aren't we supposed to eat from our own plates?"

"No, Charley. In real Italian restaurants everyone eats from the same dish."

So I dig in, well sort-of. I twirl the long noodles with my fork as gracefully as I can and try not to be messy. For once I'm actually self-conscious about eating in front of someone. I thought that was a paranoia only the Pretty Posse members possess. Strange, huh?

It's the best spaghetti I've ever eaten, and that's saying something, considering every time Mrs. Giovanni hosts the Sunday Night Suppers she makes the same type of pasta. All throughout dinner the large wood radio in the restaurant plays classy Italian music. It switches between opera music and singers like Frank Sinatra and Dean Martin. The meatballs are delicious, and I can't help but wish dinner would never end.

I'm not paying attention as I slurp up a long strand of spaghetti, until I realize Frankie is eating the same noodle at the other end. We both chuckle nervously as the pasta breaks in the middle. My cheeks turn the color of a tomato and I look down at my lap.

"You have some sauce on your chin," Frankie points out. I quickly wipe it off. Why do I feel so embarrassed over these little insignificant things?

Finally there's only one meatball left. Frankie pushes it with the back of his fork toward my side of the plate. I realize this is one of his many attempts to act like a gentleman, so even though I'm absolutely stuffed, I eat it. A few minutes later, Frankie's Uncle Salvatore and his Grandpa Luigi come out of the kitchen. His uncle is holding an accordion and his grandpa has a mandolin. I think I know what's going to happen next, but it's still a spectacular surprise to hear them sing and play a song called:

"Bella Notte"

❧

Oh, this is the night,

It's a beautiful night

And we call it Bella Notte

Look at the skies

They have stars in their eyes

On this lovely Bella Notte

Side by side

With your loved one

You'll find enchantment here

The night will weave

Its magic spell

When the one you love is near!

Oh, this is the night

And the Heavens are right!

On this lovely Bella Notte

(J.Francis Burke, Peggy Lee. 1955)

The rest of the night is like right out of *Lady and the Tramp*. I guess the night was *supposed* to be like the movie. After dinner, Frankie and I go on a late night stroll through the park. We hold hands as we silently walk down the cobblestone path, under a sky of stars and an enormous full moon illuminating the sky. It's warm, probably around 70 degrees. I couldn't have asked for a more beautiful night. But then again, that's what Bella Notte means; beautiful night. I can hear the crickets chirping in the bushes, and fireflies glow randomly throughout the park.

"Let's go to the hill," I say quietly, breaking the peaceful silence, "we can catch the most fireflies up there." He nods and I pick up the pace a little to get there quicker. I pass by the old stomping ground, the baseball diamond, for the last time, bidding it farewell in my mind. At the top of the hill, Frankie lays down in the cool grass, with his arms crossed beneath his head, staring off into the sky. I sit down next to him and flip onto my stomach, my chin cupped in my hands, legs bent at the knees, folding upward and crossed.

"What happened to catching fireflies?" he asks. There *are* a lot more up here than down below.

"I guess I just didn't feel like it," I shrug. I hope it's not too apparent that I just made up an excuse to go on top of the hill.

"I…I think I know how Ricky felt…the first time he took Penny on a date."

"What do you mean?"

"I mean that he didn't, like, want to talk about it…it was some huge secret or something. And for days afterwards he just, kind-of, stayed in his room. Only came out for meals, and even then didn't eat nearly as much as normal. It was really…I don't know…weird."

"I'm glad they're getting married. I mean, really, it was about time they did. I'm just upset I'm going to miss it."

"I'll send you pictures once I know what you're new address is."

"Let's not talk about me moving. I don't want to think about leaving tomorrow. I just want to enjoy the here and now."

"Oh. I didn't mean to bring it up. Sorry."

"That's alright. Hey, why don't we play a game? In the game, we have to name the two people who will most likely end up together. Like, Ricky and Penny. Or Jack and Petunia."

"JC and Marilyn Monroe." I laugh at this one.

"Anthony Giovanni and Ella Walters," I predict.

"Max and Sophie O'Neal. I hear the girl can cook." I smile at his comment.

"Biff Richardson and Nathaniel Collins." Frankie grins and jokes, "I think you're on to somethin'. There's a reason those two are always off on their own, supposedly 'scheming' together."

"Larry and Margaret Hanson."

"Danny and Catherine Foley."

"Arthur and Heather Honeyduke. What can I say? He's a sucker for a blonde."

"Jon Thompson and Elizabeth Scott."

"Mickey and Mary Wells."

"José Rodriguez and Christina Galstavi."

"Me,"

"and,"

"you." We say it at the same exact time. There's a long silence that follows. I take a deep breath. I know what I'm about to do, so I need all the courage I can summon within me. My stomach is filled with butterflies, my mouth is dry, and my heart is racing.

"I'm going to kiss you now. And there's nothing in the world that's going to stop me," I state seriously. I put my face right up to his before I can have second thoughts. I close my eyes, and…

My watch starts beeping. Of *course*.

"Time to take you home," he sighs. I think I hear a trace of disappointment in his voice.

"I know. I've got an early start tomorrow."

CHAPTER 20

Good Bye

The next morning I'm awake bright and early, 5 am, absolutely bushed yet dressed and ready to load every box into the moving truck. The McDougals, who've been camping out in a tent in our backyard since they arrived, help us load everything. It's weird seeing the interior of my house stark empty, yet the front yard is overflowing with crates and cardboard containers.

The McDougals came a few days early so they could come to my party, though their truck doesn't arrive until this afternoon. Wisconsin's a lot farther away than New York, so no wonder it's taking so long to get here.

The boys show up and start helping us with stuff like mattresses, couches and dressers. Grandma and Grandpa don't help that much, but that's just because they're old and we don't want them to hurt themselves moving anything too heavy. With all the combined efforts, we're finished loading everything about an hour ahead of schedule. I take a quick break to eat my breakfast, which consists of exactly one banana.

By 10:00 am, Yank and Ginger are already loaded in the car, Grandpa's truck bead is full of furniture strapped tightly down, and everyone's waiting for us to drive away.

I exchange good byes and many, many hugs as the end of my last summer here approaches. My parents and grandparents get in their automobiles. They pull out of the driveway and onto the street, where I'm standing, giving my last goodbyes. Father honks the horn.

"Come on Charlotte! We have to go!" Mother shouts. I turn and walk towards the car, tears about to stream from my eyes, when Frankie exclaims, "Wait, Charley! You forgot something!"

I turn around, imagining what I could have possibly forgotten, when before I know it he's wrapped his arms around me and pulled me in and there we are, kissing. Actually kissing. Right there infront of the team and my family, but I don't even think about that. It's impossible to think about anything. I completely forget where I am, my heart seems to have stopped and my stomach is fluttering but I barely notice because I feel that usual electric shockwave, except this time it's completely filled my body. Finally I pull back but immediately regret it because I didn't want the kiss to end so soon. I'm so dizzy and I feel like I'm in a dream.

I hobble dazedly into the backseat of my car and turn around in my seat. As we drive off I wave out the back window to the best friends I've ever known and the love of my life, the tears just now beginning to trickle down my cheeks. I wave until they disappear down the street, just a miniscule blur in the distance, while I head into an uncertain future. Good bye, Valia Springs. Goodbye, Frankie. Goodbye.

The ideas for this story came to me after watching *The Sandlot* for the first time on a cold Friday in school in January of 2010. After I got home from school I immediately grabbed a pen and a notebook and began writing ideas. Originally, the story was going to be about my pathetic obsessive love for a boy in my class (when I was in sixth grade) and how he was pathetically obsessively in love with a girl in the grade above ours. Unfortunately, that part of the story would've been true. The other contents of the story would've been completely fictitious, such as my grade not having a softball team so I would have to join my grade's baseball team. Of course, the same boy I was in love with would be the team captain, best player on the team, cool, popular, good-looking (sounding familiar?), etcetera. Through the course of that story, he would gradually begin to develop feelings for me and eventually we would end up together (by the way, that *never* would've happened in real life). There was going to be a whole bunch of other nonsense going on in the background, like how I would finally stand up to a boy that was bullying me by beating him up, only to have detention after school on the same day of our baseball team's championship game. But other than those ideas

I just named, I literally couldn't come up with anything else. The original path I was going down felt so limited to what was my world at the time, and there really wasn't much room for fiction at that point.

So I decided to change it up a little bit. Why not write a story about an outcast tomboy living in the 1950's, who's in love with baseball (as well as her best friend) and finds out that she only has one summer left in the town she lives in to make her mark? I decided to go with it. It seemed like a good bet, considering all I had to do was make the main character almost exactly like me (physically or otherwise), with a few distinguishable differences (such as the character being left-handed, because I am *extremely* right-handed, and the character is an only child, where as I was an only child for all of 2.5 years of my life, the character moves five times throughout the book series, where I have lived in one house for my whole existence, I don't live in either New York or Georgia, and I wasn't born anywhere near the 1950s. I could go on a lot further with the differences, but it would get way too boring).

I think the biggest change I made when I took the notebook story and began to type it was changing the main character's name. Yes, originally it wasn't Charlotte nicknamed Charley, it was Nicole nicknamed Nick. Unfortunately, Nicole was far too uncommon of a name back then for it to be historically accurate, so it had to be changed. Plus, I recently discovered that the name Charlotte means 'feminine' in French. Perfect, huh? I LOVE the irony of it. The year the story took place in went from 1953 to 1954 to, finally, 1955. Arthur was much more of a background character in the first draft, but I realized he had to be brought out of the darkness. He was too important to not be given a bigger role. Finally, the book was originally supposed to be one large volume, which I later decided to split into Part I and Part II, which would be separate books. But it wasn't long until Part I and II became Books 1 and 3 in a four book series. I felt like I needed to squish a story between them, and then conclude the trilogy with a final installment, for readers to get the full effect of the novels. Thus there will be four books. Keep your eyes open for the second book in the series, "The Last Time." It will be coming soon.

ACKNOWLEDGEMENTS

I would love to say a big thank you to all of my friends who I may or may not have forced to read the original hand-written copy of this story in my cocker-spaniel notebook. I love you all so much! But probably the most loyal reader of them all was the awe-inspiring musician/future Taylor Swift, Emma Malik. Thanks for being my best constructive critic and encourager for my story. We both know it had to be told one way or another! I'd like to thank the movie *The Sandlot* for inspiring me to write this. The first time I watched that movie it was a Friday in school in January of seventh grade, and it was Emma's first time watching it, too. We both were freaking out at how awesome the movie was and it will forever be our all-time favorite movie! Adding to this, I have to thank my friend Maloree Perkins-Kriewall for fighting with Emma over who got to read my writing first. You made me feel special! I need to thank my fifth and sixth grade English/History/Homeroom teacher, Ms. Albrecht (who will be a married woman and will no longer have that last name by the time she reads this) for also reading the notebook version of this and claiming that she liked it. I have to thank my sixth grade Math and Science teacher, Mr. Anetrini, for letting me borrow his last name. Oh, what the heck! I'll just thank these wonderful teachers that I had in junior high, as well, for their wonderful encouragement: Mrs. Madonia, Ms. Kiernicki, Mrs. Megge, and Mrs. Falk. I *must* thank a girl in my seventh and eighth grade class (who I will not name) for telling me that my book was boring. At least she was being honest. I have to thank one of my best friends, Savannah Bolda, for being an enthusiastic listener that one day when I told her the general plotline of all four books. I am *definitely* going to sign her copies of all four of them! I have to thank one of my other best friends, Lily Dunnigan, for helping me come up with the ideas for the second book of this series while we were jumping on her trampoline. Apparently trampolines are great at helping us come up with story ideas!

Of course I'll thank my parents for being encouraging and supportive of my writing, and my two little sisters, Kylee and Kristyn, for distracting me the whole time I was trying to type this book. Thanks for forcing me to play with you once in a while, because too much typing can definitely be a bad thing! Also, Kylee, who happens to be obsessed with the character Petunia McDougal, needs to be reassured that Petunia will come back again in *at least* one more book in this series. I quote Kylee, "I love her! She's so FUNNY!!!" I'll thank my Grandma Pat for having me read this to her multiple times because she kept forgetting everything I'd read to her before. If it wasn't for her, I wouldn't know how this book sounded when I read it out loud. I'll thank my

Grandma Joanie and Grandpa Chester for inspiring the role of Charley's grandparents in this book. Although the two of you aren't exactly like the grandparents in this story, you're such stereotypical American grandparents that I just *had* to represent you in the book (of course I mean that in a good way!). Grandpa, you've told me so many stories about your life that I just HAD to include one...so for the record, I used the story about how your mother was *almost* a nun, and you were *almost* a priest. I want to thank Jack, Kenny and Seth Wojcik, my brothers who aren't actually related to me, for trying to read the first two chapters of the notebook version of this on literally my second day of writing it. Your tolerance was greatly appreciated. In conclusion, I need to thank Diane, Margie and Charles, the three adults who I (along with my mom) backpacked in the Grand Canyon with for four days in April 2011. Thanks for not getting sick of me constantly having to take a break or get my blisters under control. I know you all specifically asked to be mentioned in this book, so here you go. If I could pick anybody to go backpacking with, it would be you three. And last but never least, I need to thank God for blessing me with my writing capabilities. Without them, no one would be reading this.

Love always,

Jacky

Watch for the release of these upcoming books by Jacquelyn Eubanks:

The Last Time

The Last Chance

The Last Doubt

Visit

www.JacquelynEubanks.com

and don't forget to LIKE us on FaceBook at **The Last Summer**.